THE EVERLASTING ROAD

THE EVERLASTING ROAD

WAB KINEW

tundra

Tundra Books, an imprint of Tundra Book Group, a division of Penguin Random House of Canada Limited

Publisher's note: This book is a work of fiction. Names, characters, places and incidents either are the product of the author's imagination or are used fictitiously, and any resemblance to actual persons living or dead, events, or locales is entirely coincidental.

LIBRARY AND ARCHIVES CANADA CATALOGUING IN PUBLICATION

Title: The everlasting road / Wab Kinew.
Names: Kinew, Wab, 1981- author.
Identifiers: Canadiana (print) 2021035223X | Canadiana (ebook) 20210352248 |
    ISBN 9780735269033 (hardcover) | ISBN 9780735269040 (ebook)
Classification: LCC PS8621.I54 E94 2022 | DDC jC813/.6—dc23

Published simultaneously in the United States of America by Tundra Books of Northern New York, an imprint of Tundra Book Group, a division of Penguin Random House of Canada Limited

Library of Congress Control Number: 2021949358

Edited by Lynne Missen
Jacket art copyright © 2023 by Chippewar
Jacket designed by Lisa Jager
The text was set in Adobe Caslon Pro.

Printed in Canada

www.penguinrandomhouse.ca

1 2 3 4 5   27 26 25 24 23

Penguin
Random House
tundra | TUNDRA BOOKS

To the students at
Pelican Falls First Nations High School:

You inspired me to write the first book in this series,
Walking in Two Worlds.

Having the opportunity to write and publish a novel
was the realization of a long-standing dream of mine,
and you helped me to achieve it.

So to you I say "miigwech," and . . .

Ando-bawaajigek—seek your dreams!

"Just keep going. No feeling is final."
—RAINER MARIA RILKE, *BOOK OF HOURS*, I 59

Anishinaabe Terms and Pronunciation Guide

**Ahow kaa'anishinaa ndinawemaaganiidog.
Niiyogiizhik indigo. Pizhiw gosha ndoodem**
(*AH-how caw-nish-in-NAH in-din-uh-WAY-mah-
gun-ee-toke. NEE-yo-gee-shick in-di-GO. pi-SHEW
go-SHAW in-DOH-dem*): O, all of those whom I
presume to be my relatives, I invoke you. My name
is Four Skies and I am a member of the Lynx Clan.

Ahow Wiisinidaa! (*AH-how wee-sin-it-TAH*): Let's eat!

Anishinaabe (*a-nish-in-NAH-bay*): Ojibwe or
Indigenous

Anishinaabe Akiing (*a-nish-in-NAH-bay AH-king*):
Anishinaabe territory

Anishinaabeg (*a-nish-in-NAH-bake*): Plural of
Anishinaabe.

Doodemi'aatig (*TOE-tem-ee-ah-tig*): A wooden-pole grave marker bearing the insignia of the person's clan.

Een say (*EEN say*): Not words per se, but an expression used to signal pity with a humorous connotation.

Eniwek igo kiga'onji-pimaadiz ndiwe'igan (*AY-knee-wake EE-go key-gohn-jih-pee-MAH-tizz in-tay-WAY-gun*): Through my drum you will live just a little bit longer.

Gaagigewekinaa (*kah-key-gay-WAY-kin-nah*): The Everlasting Road

Gego zegiziken (KAY-go ZAY-gizz-zee-ken): Don't be scared

Gigawaabamin minawaa (*KEY-gah-wah-bah-min min-ah-WAH*): I will see you again.

Mishi-pizhiw (*mi-SHIP-i-shoe*): A supernatural being in Anishinaabe culture

Niikaanis, niikaanis, niikaanis, Gaagigewekinaa (*KNEE-kon-iss, KNEE-kon-iss, KNEE-kon-iss, kah-key-gay-WAY-kin-nah*): The sacred form of saying "Brother, brother, brother, the Everlasting Road," shared in modified form for the purposes of this book.

Nisayenh (*ni-SIGH-yay*): My Older Brother.

Onjine (*OWN-jin-nay*): The way you behave will come back to you.

Sabikeshiinh (*SUB-kay-shee*): Spider

Waawaate (*WAH-wah-tay*): The Northern Lights

Waawaate-iban (*WAH-wah-tay-ee-bun*): A form of the above name that indicates the person is deceased.

Zhede (*SHAH-tay*): The pelican

AUTHOR'S NOTE

This novel makes reference to many Anishinaabe cultural teachings. However, the details and descriptions have been changed slightly to preserve the sanctity of the authentic Anishinaabe traditions. If these scenes resonate with you, or you are an Anishinaabe person looking to reconnect with your culture, please consider these scenes as partial encouragement to offer tobacco to an Elder or spiritual person you know in your nation or territory who can provide you with real-world guidance. These teachings come through relationships built over time. Tobacco is a sacred gift given to honor someone you want to build or advance a relationship with in the context of community, culture, or ceremony.

PROLOGUE

Bugz felt alone as she stared into the abyss. In this case staring into the abyss meant scanning an armada of enemy Clan:LESS starships that stretched as far as her eyes could see. Their numbers were without end. She was flying solo. Still, she liked her odds. As Bugz floated weightlessly in the darkness of space her peripheral vision sparkled with brilliant stars, some occasionally hidden by her long black hair swaying in zero gravity. She was dressed in the way that millions of online followers had come to expect from her: a sleek black spacesuit carved with neon-pink and Day-Glo-green floral patterns. Bugz—the myth, the legend, the ruler of the Floraverse—was ready to go to war once more against her mortal enemies.

The ships at the front of the Clan:LESS fleet inched closer to Bugz, clearly waiting for a signal to attack.

Though huge in numbers, this squad had a ragtag appearance. Some of the ships looked like military fighter jets; others she recognized from famous sci-fi sagas she'd streamed. As she searched their ranks, she even saw one that resembled the rickety old plane the Wright brothers had first flown on Earth so many years ago, the pilot exposed to the nearly absolute-zero temperature of space with only a pair of goggles and a leather cap to protect him. This was only possible because this particular showdown was taking place in the online world of the 'Verse—the Spirit World, to be specific. While the Floraverse had an augmented reality mode, or AR, which allowed players to experience the game as a layer over top of their real-world everyday locations, the Spirit World was a fully virtual realm where almost anything was possible—including a pilot like this one surviving in the vacuum of space.

Farther back in the crowd, Bugz could see massive ships shaped like pyramids and cubes, and even one that resembled a metallic moon complete with artificial crater. Bugz chuckled to herself as she ticked off the movies and series in which she'd seen each of these larger craft.

Well, Bugz thought, *Clan:LESS never claimed to be creative.*

As formulaic as these larger, distant ships may have been in design, they were still dangerous in practice. Any one of them could destroy Bugz. She swiped open a magnification window and watched these craft empty their guts of thousands of smaller attack ships, which joined the torrent flooding toward her. She reached for the computer on her wrist and hacked into the Clan:LESS voice-com channel. Through the vulgar babble of sexist and anti-Indigenous comments came a voice that Bugz could never forget.

"Alright, men," the voice announced, pausing to allow the chatter on the line to die down. "Activate your weapons and get ready to attack on the count of three . . ."

Alpha. It was all Bugz could do to stifle the sick feeling in the pit of her stomach. Alpha and his Clan:LESS followers had taken everything from Bugz in the 'Verse, including her favorite creation: the underwater serpent Mishi-pizhiw. They'd even come to her Rez in the real world and desecrated an ancient sacred site of the Anishinaabe people. Bugz breathed deeply and exhaled. She decided that the best response to Alpha and Clan:LESS in this instance, a moment in which they believed their pending attack would be intimidating, would be humor. And perhaps to cause a little mischief.

"Wait," Bugz shouted into the voice-com channel, cutting Alpha off even as he began to count. "Do you mean, like, attack on three? Or do you mean one, two, three, and then attack?"

Bugz's trolling had an instant effect. She could see the pilots of the starships closest to her scrunching their foreheads in confusion. The centurion flying the lead spacecraft raised a hand to his ear piece as though awaiting urgent clarification to this important question. A bodybuilder in a Clan:LESS fighter jet looked over to the ship to his right, searching for advice, then to his left.

Bugz tossed her head back and laughed as hard as she could, her cackle audible only to herself, the rest of her laugh lost forever in the abyss of space. Messing with Clan:LESS never got old, no matter how outmatched she was in a showdown.

"You idiots!" Alpha shouted over the voice channel. "It doesn't matter. Just attack!"

The bodybuilder and the centurion made eye contact, still unsure of what to do.

Alpha screamed "ATTACK!"

At this, thousands of Clan:LESS ships surged across Bugz's field of view. They began charging their weapons systems, banking off into complicated flight patterns, and, in a few instances, crashing into each other.

Bugz fired up her jetpack and shot straight up from her original position at a breakneck speed. She leaned forward to bank her flight path over top of the Clan:LESS horde, who kept flying together across a relatively horizontal plane. As Bugz flew overhead, she had her pick of which craft to strike with her laser gun. A star fighter here. A stealth bomber there. The Wright brothers plane thrown in for good measure. She struck them down and the gamertags of their pilots rose slowly from their wreckages.

"zzTie_Fighterzz has been eliminated by Bugz."

"You2andEuropaToo has been eliminated by Bugz."

"WrightStuff has been eliminated by Bugz."

From the rear of the Clan:LESS formation, a long column of star fighters peeled off from the squad and arced up toward Bugz, firing lasers at her along the way. As they closed in on her position, their barrage grew more and more accurate until some shots crashed into Bugz's suit and forced her to change course. She could take only so much of this fire.

Bugz banked off in a curved flight path back toward the horde, who now appeared above her. She moved her arms down to her sides, which made her look like an eagle diving for her prey. As she hurtled toward the mass of Clan:LESS ships, the elite fighters on her tail proved dangerous to their own clanmates. With every shot they took at Bugz and missed—and there were many of these stray laser beams—they destroyed one of their own. Dozens of gamertags rose from the wreckage before Alpha shouted over the voice channel for the elite star fighters to stop the friendly fire.

Bugz punched through the sea of Clan:LESS ships like a diver into water, the wake from her jetpack tracing a path behind her for her enemies to follow. The light from a nearby star flared on Bugz's visor and lit her up in a brilliant purple hue. The scene was one of pure beauty, prompting Bugz to take a screenshot—until, of course, she cleared the ships and the firing resumed.

From here, the discipline of the Clan:LESS ranks broke down.

Bugz charted a course like a pinball through the growing asteroid field of high-tech Clan:LESS wreckage. It took all of her focus to stay clear of the two Clan:LESS ships colliding in front of her while keeping an eye on the fighter firing at her from her six. Along the way, she dished out a few laser blasts at a craft pulling up beside her. The barrage of laser fire, exploding ships, and chaos illuminated everything around her. The heat, light, and danger were all closing in. Bugz gritted her teeth, braced for impact, and desperately scanned her surroundings for an opening. Looking behind herself, down, and to the left, she saw it—a small patch of darkness—an escape route.

Bugz swiveled across three dimensions and cranked her jetpack to full speed.

She shot out of the chaos, away from the horde, and into the soothing emptiness of the universe. After a breath, she throttled back on the jetpack and turned to see how close the Clan:LESS horde was. They were giving chase, but she still had at least another moment before she needed to engage them again. The distant Clan:LESS fighters poured into a large formation like grains of sand streaming through the center of an hour glass, intending to overwhelm her with one immense, direct barrage.

Bugz locked and loaded a second laser cannon in her left hand to complement the one in her right. She raised her guns and angled the open sights toward the coming Armageddon.

Before doomsday could arrive, however, something bizarre happened to the Clan:LESS armada. Ships began spinning off from the flank of the immense crowd as though they were toys being thrown out of a toy box by a rowdy toddler. The disturbance made its way to the front of the formation with shocking speed—whatever was causing this chaos was closing in on the lead ship, and fast.

Bugz exhaled sharply and readied her weapons. The lead Clan:LESS ship exploded in a shower of blue, red, and purple sparks, its hull splitting right down the middle. Bugz pulled back on each trigger slowly, a hair's width away from unleashing overwhelming laser fire on whatever was about to emerge as the source of the devastation before her.

It registered with Bugz in an instant that whatever was behind this mess was of immense power—enough power to rampage through the Clan:LESS horde in a way that even she hadn't been able to. It occurred to Bugz that she might be about to meet her match.

As the explosion parted, a humanoid figure wrapped in a sleek black spacesuit shot through the wreckage like a bullet. It grabbed Bugz by her shoulders and flew the two of them away from the remains of Clan:LESS; they traveled at a speed so high that the light from distant stars dragged behind them, creating a shower of shooting stars.

Light speed, she thought to herself. She wondered whether the physics of the 'Verse were accurate in this respect. Whoever this was had clearly leveled up in a way that Bugz could barely comprehend.

As Bugz glanced at the arms of this stranger dragging her through space at an explanation-defying speed, she caught sight of neon-pink and Day-Glo-green floral designs running up the length of their arms and legs. These were Bugz's signature designs—everyone in the 'Verse knew that.

Anxiety sparked across Bugz's spirit and overtook her awareness.

She reached out and pulled the black visor off the stranger's head. Instantly, she gasped: she was staring at a mirror image of herself. The stranger-Bugz looked away, studying the battle they'd left behind. Bugz noticed that the stranger's hair was shorter than her own. *Why would I cut my hair?*

The stranger-Bugz finally looked up and met Bugz's gaze. Staring into her doppelgänger's eyes, the real Bugz froze—she entered a moment of pure and infinite calm.

The calm was shattered a heartbeat later as Bugz recognized the most significant difference between her and the stranger. The left side of the stranger-Bugz's face, the side that had initially been concealed as she looked back at the battle, was contorted into a grotesque snarl, reminiscent of a demon hound or the most hideous monster from the darkest horror movie Bugz had ever seen . . .

Bugz shot straight up in her bed, her room still dark.

It had all been a dream—the battle, the chase, her own gruesome twin.

And yet, while Bugz had awakened from one bad dream, she knew she still remained locked in a nightmare.

CHAPTER 1

Brother, brother, brother, the Everlasting Road. Bugz translated these words in her mind as she listened to the tiny, dark-skinned Elder grunt them in Ojibwe: "Niikaanis, niikaanis, niikaanis, Gaagigewekinaa."

Bugz looked up from her feet to see everyone she knew from the Rez packed tightly into the community center around her, their shoe-tapping and fidgeting testifying to the length of the ceremony. She glanced at the Afro-Indigenous Elder's hunched back just as he finished speaking. He began muttering in low guttural tones as he shook a tin can filled with rocks. Bugz had made this rattle earlier in the morning, peeling the label from a soup can and fixing a wooden handle through one end. The Elder kept shaking it as he shuffled in his thick-soled runners counterclockwise around the object that was the focal point of the room, the object everyone kept looking at, the object Bugz had never wanted to see: her brother Waawaate's coffin.

Bugz and her family'd had a year or so with Waawaate after his diagnosis, a tough year split between their home and the hospital, but when the end came, it had still felt way too fast. Bugz struggled to believe it . . . Waawaate was gone. In the four days since his passing, she'd kept busy, occupying herself with helping her family prepare for this funeral. She'd made the birchbark basket, cedar knife, rattle, and other ceremonial items she would send with Waawaate and the Elder would instruct him to use on his journey to the afterlife. Bugz had even beaded the new moccasins they'd placed on Waawaate's feet.

Bugz looked below the coffin and saw the poplar pole she'd fashioned earlier that morning. On one face was a simple carving of their family's clan—Zhede, the pelican—flying down toward the base of the pole. *Doodemi'aatig.* This type of object had given non-Indigenous people the phrase "totem pole," though these grave markers served a different purpose for the Anishinaabe than the tall poles made by West Coast Indigenous nations did for their peoples.

Bugz looked at the wooden box above and noted how pedestrian it seemed compared to the devastating impact it represented. Simple, smooth cedar adorned with copper-colored handles. A copper lock to fix the top closed. *Forever.*

Bugz studied the Elder again. He labored against his cane as he completed the circle, his tightly curled black hair spreading from the sides of his Native Pride ball cap like wings. Though she could not hear him for his mutterings, Bugz knew he was imparting instructions to Waawaate's spirit on what would await him on his four-day journey along the Path of Souls. Along that Everlasting Road, Waawaate would meet many trials—temptation, torment, a beautiful but immense mountain—and the Elder was carefully relating to him the teachings of how he could overcome those tests and join the ancestors in the Happy Hunting Grounds.

I can't believe I've been to so many funerals already that I know the funeral ceremony by heart. Such was Anishinaabe life in Bugz's time.

Bugz felt hungry and tired. The fluorescent lights buzzing high above—casting everything in a pale, sick light—didn't help. She'd slept only an hour or two on the floor of this same room during the wake held there the night before.

All of this must've been visible on her face when she turned to look at Feng, who sat beside her. He forced a smile and reached out to hold her hand.

Bugz accepted his hand without a word. Her weariness and grief expressed itself through this touch. She felt gross, and worried that Feng was only gripping her sweaty hand out of pity. If these self-doubts were a snowball, then Bugz spent the next twenty minutes rolling them across the freshly fallen snow of her grief until, finally, the huge line forming to view Waawaate a final time presented her with an opportunity to let go of Feng's hand.

Bugz scanned the crowd. She noticed Stormy wiping tears from her eyes near the back of the line. Her friend Chalice consoled her. Even in tears, Stormy looked beautiful, Bugz thought, her beauty enhanced by the knowledge that Stormy had visited Waawaate right through to the end.

Doesn't matter, Bugz thought to herself. Nothing mattered to her at the moment.

For the next hour, Bugz quietly cursed anyone who cried. What gave them the right to shed tears for the brother she missed so dearly? She nodded without expression when anyone came to offer a fist bump, and she refused to reciprocate any offered hugs, instead standing stiffly as she allowed the other party to wrap their arms around her. Finally, as the line exhausted itself, she joined her mother and father at the side of the coffin.

Bugz heard her mother sob and felt her father wrapping them both in a tight hug. She could feel him shudder, as though he were crying through his grip.

Bugz looked at her brother's hands and suddenly realized there was no way they could be Waawaate's . . . they were too plastic-looking and pale. She ran her hand over his hair. The smooth feel on her fingers reminded her of the countless times she'd braided his hair at pow-wows before he'd danced and thrilled the crowds.

When Bugz finally looked to his face, she saw that everything was wrong. He looked at once too skinny and too bloated. His permanent smile had been replaced by a flat expression, the sides of his mouth sinking into his cheeks. His overall appearance was one of lethargy, not of the vitality and exuberance that had characterized him until his final breath. She cursed the funeral home. *Bunch of hacks.*

Shaking her head, Bugz felt the weight of the past year pulling on her.

"Okay," her father said. "Okay."

Nodding her head slightly, Bugz leaned into the casket and kissed Waawaate on the forehead. The cold, flat feel of his skin surprised her.

"Gigawaabamin minawaa Nisayenh," Bugz whispered. *I will see you again, my Older Brother.*

CHAPTER 2

Bugz rifled through the drawer in the kitchen just off of the community center's main hallway. She scraped her fingers along the cheap plywood bottom quickly as she searched desperately for the tool she needed to help herself feel better. Not finding what she wanted, Bugz slammed the drawer shut with a jangle of metal.

"Can I help you, Buggy?" Bugz's aunt Spring asked. The older Anishinaabe woman wiped her hands on her apron, signaling to the others in the kitchen that she was taking a break from preparing the feast that would follow the funeral. Spring ran the back of her brown hand across her glistening forehead.

Bugz furrowed her brow and quickly opened and slammed shut a number of other drawers. "It's fine. I just need a sharp knife," she said, without making eye contact.

Her aunt pursed her lips. "Plenty of knives in the top drawer."

"No, I need a sharper one." Tears stained Bugz's eyes red. She pulled the top drawer open again, took out a large butcher knife, held it to the light, and then bolted out the kitchen door. Her aunt hollered after her, but by the time Spring reached the hallway, Bugz had already locked herself in one of the restrooms down the hall.

Bugz drew in a deep breath and let it out in a huff. When she saw her reflection, with its wet eyes framed by dark circles, the source of her sorrow—her older brother's departure—flooded back into her thoughts. She felt this tidal wave of grief so intensely that she was somewhat surprised when the person staring back at her from the mirror was not washed away. Instead, Bugz sneered at herself and pushed out a stuttering breath. She knew there would be neither a quick fix nor any dramatic change to the way she felt now. This was her new reality.

A pounding at the door snapped Bugz's attention quickly to the left. She shouted, "What?"

"It's Auntie. What are you doing in there?"

"Nothing," Bugz lied. She sniffed and cleared her throat as her aunt regrouped.

"Well, why did you take the knife in there?" A softer knock at the door. "Buggy, I'm worried about you. It's tough for all of us and—"

"It's okay, Auntie." Bugz held the knife to the mirror and rotated it in front of herself. The fluorescent light flared on the blade. She felt bad for scaring her aunt—Bugz knew that her mother had told her aunt about some of Bugz's past struggles, and her aunt was probably worried Bugz might harm herself. Bugz tossed her head forward quickly and with her free hand wrapped her long black hair up as though she was going to make a ponytail. Bugz stood straight and pulled her hair along the left side of her face until her hand was just below her chin. She raised the blade. An image from her nightmare—of her doppelgänger with short hair—flashed in her mind. "I'm just cutting my hair." She heard her aunt curse, a sound of relief, from the other side of the door.

Bugz tried to run the big dull blade through her hair, but her locks offered surprising resistance. She sawed it back and forth, biting her lip with the effort. The knife seemed to tear the raven-colored strands rather than cut them. Bugz grimaced as though in pain. This was going a lot more slowly and a lot less dramatically than she'd initially imagined. In her mind's eye, when she'd imagined doing this during the start of the funeral, she'd pictured herself cutting her hair in one fell swoop, leaving herself holding a large scalp lock the size of a braid of sweetgrass. After she finally shore the first strands clear from the rest, Bugz looked to her hand expectantly, only to find herself holding a small tuft of hair no bigger than a rabbit's foot. So much for catharsis.

Another knock at the door.

"What?" Bugz asked.

"It's your aunt." Bugz imagined a smile on her auntie's face. "I brought scissors, for crying out loud. Open the door and smarten up."

Bugz bounded to the door, relieved, leaving the knife in the sink. The moment she unlocked the door her aunt pushed her way in and glanced at the tuft of hair in her hand. "Een say, is that all you cut off?" she said in mocking voice. "If you're going to chop off all your hair, at least make sure you cut off enough so that people will notice." She wrapped her strong, warm hands around Bugz's shoulders and centered her in front of the mirror again. "Besides, at this pace you'll be in here all day. And there's already a line forming to get in."

Quickly, Spring set to work cutting Bugz's long hair, using the same familiar movements Bugz had witnessed in the kitchen just a short time ago as her aunt had sliced and diced moose meat, potatoes, and vegetables. As Spring worked, she spoke in a calm voice that Bugz remembered from her childhood, when Spring used to read her bedtime stories while babysitting.

"You know, as Anishinaabe people, traditionally we'd cut our hair when we lost somebody we cared about. While people may not do it as often today, I respect the fact you're trying to honor that tradition." A look of determination covered her aunt's face.

Bugz felt her aunt tug and pull on her scalp. As she did, she thought back to that first Sweat Lodge ceremony when her brother Waawaate had fallen ill, literally collapsing unconscious in front of all the other people there. Bugz recalled how she'd felt so protective of her brother—so protective that she'd broken a number of ceremonial taboos just so she could rush to his side, cradle his head, and try to nurse him back to health. She remembered how her hair had fallen across his face, as though shielding him from what tormented him. But it hadn't worked, and now Bugz had to cut that same hair off. It had failed her. She had failed him. Bugz shook her head at the thought, and this earned a scolding from her aunt.

"It was one of the only times the Ancient Ones would cut their hair. When they were grieving they'd cut their hair to signal they were entering a new stage of their lives." A smile spread back across Spring's face. "Of course, they'd actually make it count, though, not like your little baby cuts."

"Shut up, Auntie." Bugz felt her face reddening, and she couldn't help remembering the way her brother would tease her, joke with her, and make her laugh. Even as he lay emaciated in the hospital bed, too weak to open a Pepsi bottle, he'd still had enough energy to crack a joke. Bugz smiled through new tears welling in her eyes. Her aunt pulled Bugz's hair back, assessed her work so far, and set the scissors in motion again. As she did, she hummed a bittersweet melody that Bugz recognized as a pow-wow tune. *No*, she corrected herself. It was an older sacred song you wouldn't hear at a pow-wow, only in ceremony. The last time she'd used it was when she sang it to her brother in that hospital room. She joined in with her aunt and harmonized the last half of the song, dragging out the vocables at the end in a soulful, mournful way. She sniffed.

"Last time I sang that song was to Waawaate, right when he crossed over," Bugz said softly.

"I'm sorry, baby." Her aunt paused. "It's a good one. A healing song."

"Didn't work." Bugz looked to her shoes.

"You don't know that." Spring's voice was suddenly serious. "You don't know what your brother went through. What he's going through now." She met Bugz's eyes in the mirror. "Your song helped him on his journey. I know it did." She leaned in and wrapped Bugz in a deep embrace. Wiping her cheeks, Spring ran her hands through Bugz's hair a few more times, studying the way it bounced back from different angles in the mirror. When she was satisfied with what she saw, she spoke again.

"Our hair represents our spirits." Spring forced a smile. "And now it's time for your spirit to start over again."

CHAPTER 3

Bugz took the hair clippings she'd gathered from the gray tile floor of the bathroom and burned them in the ceremonial fire outside the community center. She prayed for her brother as she watched the black hair disappear quickly into ember. When she walked back inside, her dad simply nodded, acknowledging her new shorter locks. He understood. The rest of the day flew by in a series of fragmented scenes Bugz knew she would never forget . . . embers in the fire.

A crowd around a grave singing a memorial song until everyone's voice was hoarse.

The black and white ribbons on the shoulders of the pallbearers fluttering in the wind as the coffin was lowered.

Bugz's father stepping to the edge of the hole in the earth and screaming with all the air in his lungs, "Waawaate! Waawaate! Waawaate!"

Her mother embracing him as he finished.

The youngest pallbearer jumping down into the grave. The sound of him hammering the nails to close the wooden box that surrounded the coffin.

The pace of the day seemed to slow as the Black-Anishinaabe Elder commanded everyone not to look at the grave site as they left. "We must never cross the line that separates the living from the dead. Respect that dividing line. So when you leave here, don't look back. Only forward." All in attendance dutifully obeyed the little old man. Bugz studied his mocha skin and prominent cheekbones. He looked as though he were in his nineties. Bugz wondered what it'd been like for this Elder growing up on his Rez decades ago, embodying the different parts of his identity. Her mind wandered to her own experiences being bullied. Bugz grimaced as she recalled comments about her appearance and her obsession with gaming.

Bugz's mom leaned in, interrupting her thoughts, and said "he was spotted at a young age by Elders in our area. They saw he was gifted, a prodigy. They raised him immersed in our spirituality." Perhaps that's why he'd spent the morning lying down in a room at their house . . . saving his energy to share his gifts with the mourners. Bugz nodded to herself and went to help the Elder to their truck, grateful her brother Waawaate's final instructions came from such a wise teacher.

Bugz's day resumed its rapid pace as they arrived at the feast and giveaway back at the crowded community center. Bugz usually loved moose meat, but she found the moose on her plate to be dry, disgusting, and tough. Dishes she usually considered delicacies, like rice pudding and frybread, held no interest for her.

She watched her father giving away Waawaate's rifles and pow-wow regalia to close friends and relatives. While her father was distributing the giveaway items, Bugz pocketed a Dreamcatcher that had hung above Waawaate's bed since he was a baby—a small wooden hoop, woven with red and blue thread, made to look like a spider's nest. It was supposed to keep the nightmares away. *It doesn't seem to be working now*, Bugz thought.

The crowd filed out one by one with hugs and kisses and promises to "see each other soon," though Bugz knew instantly these words would not be honored.

An awkward silence fell on the people tending to the fire when she went outside to offer tobacco.

And finally, there was the quiet that settled over the community hall once she and Feng had finished stacking plastic chairs at the end of the day.

Bugz drew in a deep breath and leaned back to take in the dull fluorescent lights as she exhaled. She sensed this moment was an opportunity to engage in deep contemplation of the nature of life, creation, and the quest to understand its significance. But she was so disgusted with the universe that she refused to indulge it by considering its meaning.

Instead, she pulled out her phone, motioned for Feng to follow her, and dove into the Floraverse.

CHAPTER 4

High atop Castle Rock, a massive rock formation in a sunny part of the Floraverse, Feng nudged Bugz playfully.

"C'mon," he said, passing her and looking back as he edged closer to the juniper-lined cliff. He leaned forward, encouraging her to follow him as his feet found the lichen that marked the last steps before the steep drop.

Feng jumped high into the air, spreading his arms like eagle wings and arcing into a swan dive. This action was an inside joke of sorts, calling to mind Bugz's dive that had kicked off the pair's epic showdown against Clan:LESS in this same spot a year ago.

As Feng fell toward the lake below, he looked back again to see whether Bugz was following him. Just before the cliff's dark gray face obscured her completely from view, Feng could see Bugz still frozen on top of Castle Rock, her arms at her side and a serious look on her face.

He felt like he'd just told a joke at which no one had laughed. Feng sighed, extended his arms in front of him, and tore into the crystal-clear waters of Raven Lake.

Surfacing a canoe's-length away from where he'd entered, Feng rolled over and sprayed water out of his mouth, doing his best impression of a whale blasting mist from his blowhole. He fell into a lazy backstroke and looked up at the giant rock hill.

At its base were the boulders beneath which Bugz had crushed the last of the Clan:LESS resistance. They'd put up a heck of a fight, the soldiers firing a seemingly never-ending torrent of bullets and laser beams from their positions, screaming to one other amidst the raging fury. Feng had known exactly what his former clanmates had planned. He'd heard them discuss it, back when he was still one of their brothers. They wanted to go out on their shields like Spartans, battling with their backs to one another until they could fight no longer. They'd expected a hero's finish, with each of them inflicting as much damage on Bugz as they could until they were slowly and gloriously exhausted of ammunition and the will to fight.

Instead, Bugz had silenced all of their war cries in an instant. Once she'd mastered the art of controlling rocks, stones, and boulders, Bugz had simply summoned an avalanche and buried the clan beneath massive dark stones jumbled on top of each other like firewood in the back of a pickup truck. The battle had ended with the snap of a finger.

It had taken Feng's former clanmates Gym, Behemoth, and Joe months to respawn in the Spirit World after that. Their leader, Alpha, had taken his time returning to the game too, challenged by how much his reputation had suffered thanks to another defeat at Bugz's hands. Yet he was a formidable adversary all the same. Regardless of what the fickle tastes of social media said, Feng knew that Alpha was still the second-best player in the world, after Bugz, of course.

Alpha had slowly restarted the project of rebuilding the "clan that was not a clan." From time to time, Feng would see updates about how their followers were growing in number or how they'd acquired some new piece of weaponry; to Feng, it all seemed to be counting down to their next encounter. No matter how long the wait, Feng knew they'd meet on the battlefield again. And the more time that passed, the more Feng felt this threat looming large.

Feng's gaze ran up the side of the rock face, and past more evidence of the battle. Debris from the Clan:LESS helicopters was fused grotesquely into the side of Castle Rock, the heat of explosions having melded them permanently with the stone they'd crashed into. Even the pilots and gunners were still visible in some spots, frozen forever in time as tributes to Bugz's mastery. Feng looked up past other clan members trapped by petrified vines, set that way under the battle's debris and ash after being enveloped by Bugz's plant allies.

Feng scanned up to the top of the cliff and beheld her, the undisputed ruler and queen of the Floraverse, looking exactly as she did in the real world: Bugz, in a black hoodie, her shorter hair fluttering in the wind. In this virtual world where everyone presented an idealized version of themselves and covered up the parts of their appearances they considered flaws, Bugz's re-creation of her real-world appearance was a sign of her confidence, a sign of defiance even. She was so good at the game she didn't have to conform. It hadn't always been that way, of course. It had taken Bugz years to push past the superficial influencer-type skins and to present herself in the 'Verse as she was in the real world, including the parts of her appearance Feng knew she was self-conscious about. Bugz stood perfectly still, studying him, the midday sun glowing brilliantly behind her like a halo.

"Coming?" he called to her. After a pause long enough to make Feng feel self-conscious—maybe she was *too* confident, he thought to himself—she shook her head slowly from side to side. Feng heard her yelling back, but couldn't make the sounds out for the water he was splashing in. "What?" he called as he grew still.

"Let's go," Bugz shouted, as clear as the day.

CHAPTER 5

Bugz shot through the air like a bullet, dragging Feng behind her across the blue of the virtual sky. After arcing toward the horizon, far beyond Raven Lake and many nearby tributaries, the pair tore into Lake of the Torches and sped through the emerald abyss of its waters. This mystical place had always served as Bugz's headquarters, resembling the lakes near her home in the real world with its rocky shores and murky depths. But since Clan:LESS had taken it over and then Bugz had won it back more than a year ago, Lake of the Torches had become a tourist trap in the Floraverse. Thousands of 'Versonas crowded here every day, each trying to see the mythic respawn point that Bugz and Clan:LESS had warred over in one of the biggest livestreamed events in the history of the 'Verse.

As Bugz and Feng swam deeper, they passed a pair of Valkyries in scuba gear who tapped each other as they recognized their warrior-goddess hero. Before they had the nerve to ask for selfies, Bugz swam furiously and sped deeper still.

Bugz turned sharply and, with a frog-like kick of her legs, darted behind a giant stone column, pulling Feng in behind her. She waved at the lake bed and a wall of rocks swirled up around them, concealing the pair completely. The Valkyries swam by within inches of their hiding place, none the wiser. Bugz grinned at Feng, who nodded. In the low light, she studied his strong jaw and round cheeks. *He looks like he could be Anishinaabe*, she thought.

Once the warrior women were out of sight, Bugz emerged from behind the rock shroud and motioned for Feng to follow her discreetly, before the crowd gathering ahead noticed them.

The tourists were taking screenshots around a giant stone circle that looked to be Mishi-pizhiw's nest. Others in the crowd were clearly trying to activate the nest and supercharge weapons they'd brought with them, all to no avail.

"Good luck with that," Bugz said over their private voice-com channel, as much to herself as to Feng. "The thing's a decoy."

"Believe me, I remember." Feng smiled. "I was down here for every painstaking moment when you raised the lakebed." He gave her a deadpan look. "Over and over again."

Bugz softened her expression and gave him a playful nudge. Feng was a good sport. After the battles with

Clan:LESS, Bugz had felt she had no choice but to work obsessively. She knew the clan would leak the location of the nest to the world and that crowds would follow. Building a massive false rock floor and a decoy respawn point was necessary to preserve the magic of the real respawn point—Mishi-pizhiw's nest. Recalling that work, however, Bugz knew she'd pushed things too far in insisting Feng stay awake with her for two days straight to finish the job. He'd even helped get the cover story out through some of his old clan buddies. He'd told them that the magic had disappeared after the battle. No one but Feng and Bugz knew that the real nest and the tremendous power it contained were hidden deep beneath the false lake floor.

Before any of the crowd noticed them, Bugz led Feng toward a rock that looked as though it'd been split in two. The two halves parted further and swallowed Bugz and Feng whole before closing again.

In perfect darkness and total silence, the pair traveled down a submerged mine shaft passing level after level, like an elevator descending a dozen stories. If she'd wanted to, Bugz could've run her fingertips along the stone walls for reassurance—she was that close to them— but there was no need. She knew the path by heart, as well as exactly how long it would take for them to reach the bottom.

In the darkness, Bugz's mind began to wander. Immediately after the cataclysmic final showdown with

Clan:LESS, her original plan had been to rebuild her army of supernatural creatures inspired by Anishinaabe culture: Thunderbirds, sturgeon, and Mishi-pizhiw, her closest companion, who'd defended her to his death at the hands of Clan:LESS. Yet she'd done none of this . . . she'd been too preoccupied.

Bugz hadn't found time to rebuild her wealth either. Her crypto balance in the 'Verse was nearly zero. She'd abandoned selling skins, weapons, and merch to her fans. She'd stopped streaming for her followers. She'd ignored all these things that had previously made her not only the world's most famous gamer, but also a quite wealthy one, in favor of her new obsession.

In the minds of most of her old fans, she'd simply fallen off the grid. They'd moved on, now idolizing new streamers and new clans. From time to time, Bugz would see another gamer's stream getting shared with tons of likes, gifts, and micropayments from fans and she'd wonder whether she'd made a huge mistake. After all, she knew Clan:LESS or another rival group would try to attack her again soon. Her failure to build back her wealth and supernatural army made her vulnerable to a raid.

But Bugz had abandoned those things to work tirelessly on her new project, one she'd started when she'd realized her brother wouldn't be making a full recovery. This project had become the outlet for her pain. She knew without a doubt that it was her greatest creation, the most difficult thing she'd ever made in the 'Verse, and the one she'd poured more of her heart and soul into than any other—even more so than she'd done with Mishi-pizhiw.

Bugz felt Feng's hand reaching for hers, and it interrupted her thoughts. "Scared of the dark?" she asked. Hearing no reply, she decided to reassure him instead of teasing him further. "Don't worry, we've arrived."

Bugz took Feng by the hand and led him out of the mine shaft and into what she knew was a gigantic cavern, though their surroundings were still completely black. She kicked her feet slowly until her judgment told her she'd reached the center of the chamber. She let go of Feng's hand and pulled an underwater flare from her belt.

Light exploded from the capsule and burned white hot, blinding Bugz and Feng instantly.

Bugz turned her head slightly to minimize the glare as the flare burned down a bit and their eyes adjusted to its now green glow.

Suspended in the water above the real stone circle—Mishi-pizhiw's true nest—and illuminated in a murky glow was the one Bugz had come to see. The one she'd dedicated all of her time to this past year, when she could have been getting rich or building legions of majestic creatures. He was unmistakable in his grass dance regalia, which flowed like purple and green seaweed in the water's current. The face she'd known for as long as she could remember. The one she'd just said farewell to in the real world. He was right before her eyes, here in the 'Verse.

Waawaate.

CHAPTER 6

Feng watched Bugz extend her arms slowly, as though she were a holy person blessing an invisible crowd. Her eyes rolled back into her head, and were overtaken by glowing white energy that coursed furiously through her body.

Bugz leaned back and raised her arms skyward. Feng felt uneasy about what he knew she planned to do: breathe life into her creation for the first time.

Feng looked at the replica Waawaate's inert form, a slight smile spread across the virtual one's unmoving face. The resemblance was perfect—this virtual skin looked more like Waawaate to Feng than Waawaate's actual body had at the funeral. The low lime-green light of the fading flare created an eerie feeling in the cave. Feng watched as Bugz drifted higher in the water, putting more distance between her feet and the lake bed. He'd watched her come down here almost every waking hour in which she hadn't been in school or at her brother's bedside, so focused on her creation. Feng had worried it wasn't healthy, but he knew how much it meant to her, so he'd decided to keep those thoughts to himself.

He swallowed.

Suddenly, a gigantic beam of light wide enough to completely envelop the stone nest shot down from high above. The earth began to shake and the water churned and frothed. The earthquake intensified as Feng looked to the cave roof overhead; punctured as it was by the lightning strike, it looked as though it could crumble at any moment.

"Stop!" Feng yelled to Bugz. The energy continued to pour into the cave from high above, completely illuminating the replica Waawaate's still-unmoving form. Bugz remained deep in a trance, ignoring Feng, eyes still glowing white. He could see her mouth moving, as though casting a silent spell. Giant pieces of rock broke loose from the roof of the cave and sank to the lake bed, punctuating the steady rumble of the shaking earth with deep booms as they landed. A particularly jagged boulder landed hard beside Feng.

"Stop! We've got to get out of here." Feng could now see clear through the layers of the false lake bed above and make out the forms of some of the 'Versonas circling the decoy nest. It wouldn't be long before they found the true nest, with all of its power.

"Come back to me!" Bugz suddenly shouted at her re-creation of Waawaate.

"We've got to go now or they will all find Mishi-pizhiw's nest!" Feng screamed. For a moment, he thought he'd finally reached Bugz. She blinked, and the energy slowly dissipated from her eyes as she sank to the floor.

But with the earth still shaking, Feng turned to the new Waawaate and understood instantly that Bugz hadn't listened to him at all. She'd only stopped her trance because she'd accomplished her goal. The tail end of the energy beam landed and left Bugz's brother alone in its wake.

Feng watched as the figure he'd last seen mourned at a funeral seemingly returned to life. The virtual Waawaate smiled, blinked, and held his hands up in front of his eyes in amazement as the slow current pushed his green and purple regalia in a million different directions around him. Once again, Feng felt a deep sense of unease.

The tremors in the lake floor picked up speed and, without the giant energy beam in place to hold it up, the roof began to cave in.

"Let's g—"

Before Feng could completely form the words, he felt Bugz grab him by the hand and drag him violently forward. He watched, almost helplessly, as she lunged for the virtual Waawaate's hand and launched the three of them into a flight path that took them from the depths of the lake to the edge of space within seconds. As they shot by, Feng saw dozens of shocked 'Versonas swimming around the destroyed decoy nest and the rubble pile that was the collapsed lake floor, trying to make sense of what they'd just witnessed.

High above Lake of the Torches, at the edge of the virtual atmosphere—a bright planet visible below and the darkness of space visible above—Feng watched as Bugz hugged her brother's form tightly. The reunited siblings floated together in the weightlessness of infinity.

Bugz buried her head in the chest of this reborn Waawaate as a new day rose far behind them on the horizon, a dazzling sun flaring majestically against a blanket of stars. The Waawaate-bot remained still through this hug for a long breath. He blinked repeatedly, as though regaining consciousness, before leaning forward to return Bugz's virtual embrace.

CHAPTER 7

Feeling lighter than she had in recent memory, and with her heart filled with the joyful feeling of reconnecting with her brother in the 'Verse a few days prior, Bugz pushed the heavy metal door to the community hall open. Instantly she was hit with the sound of ringing bells, the up-tempo rhythm of a pow-wow drum, and the amplified voice of an emcee calling everyone to dance. The gym looked completely different from when she'd been here for her brother's funeral earlier that week. The people gathered today were talking and laughing excitedly. It was a one-day pow-wow the Rez was holding to mark the start of spring. At the center of it all was a crowd of dancers, in both regalia and street clothes, making their way around the circle in a clockwise direction.

Bugz moved forward through the crowd and past folks nodding their heads to her. She walked up to the edge of the makeshift dance arbor and felt her heart lift. She knew the song: it was an intertribal—a song calling everyone to dance. Still, Bugz held back. She'd been taught to avoid participating too soon in spiritual or cultural events while grieving. But she wasn't sure how long she was supposed to grieve. A day? A month? A year?

Rather than step out into the dancing arena, she walked over to the drum group and joined the crowd of twenty or so who'd gathered to watch the singers. As the cycle of the song began anew with a lead from one of the male singers, she watched as Stormy, Chalice, and a few other young women stood circling the men who sat singing around the drum, pounding the rhythm of the song. At the appropriate time, her friends' voices jumped in and grabbed the song, piercing the melody an octave higher than the men. Bugz hummed along but felt herself held back, perhaps by the weight of tradition, perhaps by the loneliness she felt.

Bugz turned to see past the crowd of onlookers. Like clockwork, a men's traditional dancer approached the drum, still keeping time with the beat. The crowd parted like some biblical sea and the dancer withdrew an eagle-bone whistle from beneath his shirt. He blew on it four times, the high-pitched scream evoking an eagle spinning in mid-flight, calling the drum group to sing the song four times through again. The entire spirit of the pow-wow seemed to lift, and the dancers in the circle picked up their pace. Other male dancers came forward and circled the men's traditional dancer like a breakdance cipher. He got low and showed off his moves.

Bugz felt a wave of pride wash over her mind, body, and spirit. For all she'd been through recently, including some of the heavier moments in this very room, there was nowhere she'd rather be. She shut her eyes and waited for her friends to start singing again. As they did, she pushed her voice out hard, falling into a perfect harmony with Stormy, Chalice, and the other young women. Bugz felt the melody trace its way through the air like an eagle soaring above the trees until it finally fell and trailed off with the vocables—"hey-eh-eh-yeh-yohhhhh . . ." Bugz and the other women dragged this part out, seeming to slow down time, as the lead singer kicked out his voice to start another pushup—another cycle—of the song. The drummers picked up the beat, the traditional dancer blew his whistle again, and the pow-wow's energy amped up higher still.

Fifteen minutes or so later, after several other dancers had whistled the drum group to continue singing the song—and after the arena directors had stepped in front of the drum group to close off this song and provide the singers with a break, Bugz turned and walked away from the crowd of dancers, who were exchanging fist bumps with the singers and showering them with gifts of money and tobacco. As she made her way to the emcee stand, Stormy and Chalice walked past, smiling.

"Sounding good, girl!" Stormy said through a wide grin.

"For real, though," Chalice added over her shoulder.

Bugz's heart warmed. She climbed the four stairs up the riser and stood behind the emcee, who was busy calling the order of the next few dances from his seat at a long folding table. When the emcee turned and saw her, he jumped to his feet and removed his cowboy hat from his head. Bugz studied his gray-flecked braids and the earnest look in his eyes as he extended his elbow toward her. She bumped it with her own. This was the same emcee who'd called her jingle dress contest special more than a year ago . . . back when she could afford to give a car away as first prize.

"Ms. Holiday," the emcee began. "I'm so sorry for everything you've been through. How are your mom and dad?"

"Thank you, Uncle," Bugz said, invoking the pow-wow trail practice of referring to acquaintances as relatives even when there was no blood shared. "We'll be alright."

"Yes, you will. You come from a good family." The emcee paused, signaling without words that he knew Bugz meant to ask him something.

"I was wondering if I could make a donation for a spot dance?" She pulled a hundred-dollar bill from her pocket, one she'd been given at the funeral, and extended it to him. The emcee nodded, took the money, and placed his cowboy hat back on his head. He picked the microphone back up and called to everyone in the crowded gymnasium.

"This one's going to be a spot dance, ladies and gentlemen and relatives of all genders. Young Bugz Holiday here has made a generous donation, so get out there and dance your style, and the people who end up on the spots the arena directors pick when the song finishes get the prize money." The emcee turned to Bugz, covered the mic, and asked if she wanted to do two prizes. She nodded and he returned to action. "Fifty dollars times two, so get out there and dance, and our two arena directors will find you at the end of the song."

From atop the emcee stand, Bugz could see families rising from their seats and joining the pow-wow arbor. The already crowded dance floor grew busier still. Bugz smiled, turned to the emcee, and found him grinning from ear to ear as well. It was a beautiful sight to see. Bugz remembered a time years ago when her mother had told her that whenever she felt down she should try to do something nice for someone else. Her heartbeat quickened at the memory and she found it hard to hold back tears. This pow-wow trail had been where she'd spent so much of her life with Waawaate.

"You okay, Buggy?" the emcee asked.

Bugz nodded silently and bit her lip. She took a deep breath. "Wish I could be out there."

"Well then, get out there, young lady. Nothing wrong with dancing an intertribal. We're here to have some fun and make the people proud. Besides, ask yourself—would

Waawaate go?" He smiled hard, making clear what the answer to his question was.

Bugz turned and walked down the stairs. She wondered whether her spirit was up to dancing again so soon after her brother's passing. At the foot of the staircase, she turned back to the emcee. He tipped his hat to her.

At this Bugz entered the dance arena and, after a few beats, jumped to the balls of her feet. Though she wore a hoodie and jeans, she found the jingle dress dance steps she'd known since childhood. For a moment, she lost herself in the music and her dance. She closed her eyes and soaked in the melody and the beat as she moved in time with it. Her spirit was here, fully in the moment, a feeling she hadn't had in recent memory. She felt good.

When Bugz opened her eyes, she saw Stormy smiling through her phone, which was pointed directly at her. Stormy waved and pointed at the transparent device, mouthing that she was livestreaming Bugz. Bugz smiled back to her friend. Bugz kicked her feet forward, spun quickly, and raised her left arm in the air as though holding an eagle fan. *Might as well put on a show, right?* she thought to herself.

As the pow-wow spun in a swirl of color and harmony, Bugz felt happiness fill her heart.

CHAPTER 8

The Waawaate-bot spun in time to the music, the colorful fringes of his grass dance regalia swinging and swaying like the northern lights for which he was named. He landed on his left foot with a bounce that lasted for a few beats and then spun back the other way, mirroring his dance moves in the opposite direction. As he moved, he sent waves rippling away from him across the surface of Lake of the Torches.

As Bugz watched him from the shore, singing her song on a hand drum, she entertained the thought that this virtual re-creation of Waawaate might just be as special as the real thing. She'd felt so good after dancing and singing at the pow-wow that she'd been practicing a lot with the bot in the days since. She hungered to share that feeling with the bot she'd made in her brother's image, in the image of real-life pow-wow royalty.

Bugz had breathed life into this bot with the intention of doing something no one had done before in the 'Verse—creating a fully autonomous creature, not just one who would fire out a few shots or drive a vehicle, but one that could rival a human in emotion, creativity, and complexity. Bugz could think of no activity more unique to human beings than dancing pow-wow. Waawaate slid across the lake water, dragging his toe behind, which sent a small wake running through the glass-like surface. He repeated the move on the opposite side, dragging his other toe, before landing on the pebble beach just as Bugz struck the final beat of the song.

"Stuck the landing," the Waawaate-bot said to Bugz. "Perfect balance."

"I don't know about perfect," she said with a smile as her hand drum shrank to miniature size and she returned it to her hoodie pocket.

The bot tossed his head back and laughed. "Don't be a hater. Just because I thought of dancing on the lake doesn't mean you can't do it too." He nodded convincingly. "Just make sure you give me credit when you learn how to walk on water."

Bugz shoved the Waawaate-bot's shoulder playfully. "Oh yeah. 'Attention everyone! Just so you all know, the Waawaate-AI taught me this,'" she said sarcastically.

Feng walked up along the shore, smiling and waving.

"How you folks doing?" he asked.

"We're good, brother-in-law," the bot said. Bugz noticed Feng smiling at this—perhaps even blushing. "Even now that you're here." He giggled. "'Skidding. You know I'm joking, right?"

"Yeah," Feng said as his eyes found Bugz.

Bugz felt a pang of guilt. Other than attending the one-day pow-wow in the real world, Bugz had spent all of her time with this simulation of her brother since she'd created it. Feng came when he could, but with his schoolwork and helping his aunt Liumei around the house, he had far fewer hours to spend online than Bugz. Bugz couldn't help but feel she was shortchanging him and their relationship. Truth be told, she wasn't sure exactly how to navigate the fact that they were now seeing each other. She hadn't really dated anyone before.

Before she could speak, the Waawaate-bot rose above the lake, two stories in the air. "Hey! Look at me! I. Am. Ironman!" he shouted. Bugz turned to Feng and smiled. She took his hand and lifted the pair of them up in the air to match the height of the bot. Bugz had taught herself to fly in the Floraverse and had imbued the Waawaate-bot with this skill, but she hadn't been able to transfer it to Feng, try as she might. This skill had to be earned, not learned.

"Let's do something fun," the bot shouted.

"Like what?" Bugz yelled back.

"Show him that flower thing you showed me when I first came here," Feng said to her.

"Alright," Bugz said as she closed her eyes in concentration.

A giant wave of red flowers came pouring out of the forest floor below and splashed down along the beach. The pulsating, writhing mass of crimson flora grew and spilled over itself as it raced toward the lake. Just as it reached the spot underneath Bugz, Feng, and the bot, the tsunami shot straight up into the air. Suddenly the trio was riding a vermilion roller coaster that blasted them toward the heavens before banking back to earth at a daredevil angle. As Bugz regained her bearings, she decided to send them corkscrewing over the water at a terrifying speed. All Feng could do was hang on.

The Waawaate-bot roared with laughter as the trio spun wildly. "Oh yeah? Watch this," he yelled to Bugz as they huddled close together on top of the tidal wave of poppies, red roses, and cardinal carnations. A royal-blue wave of flowers came pouring out of the forest floor as well and raced to intercept the trio. In an instant, the blue wave punched through the red one and carried Waawaate, Feng, and Bugz spiraling off into a new direction.

Bugz felt the pit of her stomach jump. She had to close her eyes to center herself again. Ever since she'd activated him in Mishi-pizhiw's nest deep below the water's surface, this virtual version of Waawaate had been able to learn every trick she'd shown him. Most of the time, as in this case, he not only learned the technique but figured out a way to do it faster and better than Bugz. It was almost scary how quickly he learned. But she wasn't about to be outdone.

Bugz refocused on the crest of red flowers and, using the power of her intuitive understanding of the blockchain gaming engine that powered the Floraverse, brought it roaring back to catch up to the bot's blue one. From then on, as in any good sibling rivalry, Bugz and the Waawaate-bot battled move for move, each trying to steer their own wave of flowers closer and quicker beneath them so they might control the group's flight path.

The combined effect of the dueling floral racers was of a tower of concentric red and blue spirals shooting up to the heavens at rocket speed. This double-helix recalled the shape of a giant strand of DNA, and it pushed the three ever higher into the clear sky above Lake of the Torches.

During the flight, Feng whispered to Bugz, "Don't you think you should rein him in? What if he gets out of control . . . a singularity sort of thing?"

Nearing the edge of space, Bugz simply smiled at Feng and looked back at the bot she was engaged in this back-and-forth with. She didn't see a virtual being or an AI, much less a threat to her online world.

Bugz only saw her brother.

CHAPTER 9

Feng's aunt Liumei ordered the teens to take a break from the 'Verse shortly after the flower battle and ushered them out of her house. After much protesting, the pair gave in and went for a walk. Feng and Bugz watched the sunset from alongside the Rez's main gravel road before wandering down to the paved walkway in front of the community's governance office.

Feng kicked a stone the size of a nickel from his path. He was filled with instant regret as he saw in the twilight the scuff mark it left on his clean, perfectly white sneakers. He felt Bugz's gaze, shot a look at her and, registering her smile, tried to make her laugh by exaggerating his scowl.

Bugz giggled and pushed him gently, her admonition more teasing than serious. "Serves you right," she said, her teeth visible through a big grin.

To Feng, at least at times like this, Bugz was perfectly beautiful, flawless in her demeanor, and blessed with a good sense of humor. He could barely prevent himself from taking flight when he got to spend time with Bugz like this. So he did what he always did when he felt this good: he started to act up.

"Nah, doesn't bother me," Feng said, making his voice sound deeper and puffing his chest out in mocking macho behavior. "See?" Feng arched his eyebrow and hopped forward. As he landed he kicked another stone forward, scuffing his white shoes a second time in the process. Bugz shook her head. The stone projectile rang off of a nearby metal surface and Feng's attention snapped toward the source of the sound.

Sitting directly outside the front doors of the office building, separated from the entryway by a blacktop driveway and framed by a collection of flags representing many local jurisdictions, was a large statue that Feng had driven by many times but never before taken the time to study.

Two large bronze moccasins the size of small cars, each with the stocky proportions of a child's shoe, were arranged one on top of the other. They sat on top of a concrete platform, as though some giant child had just taken them off and left them by the front door of their home. Though Feng was taller than most of the other kids in the local high school, he had to crane his neck up to examine them when he stood at the platform's base. He ran his hands along their smooth surface. He glanced at Bugz before scaling the platform and hugging the front of one of the slippers to keep from falling off the dais. He registered the bumpy textures of the intricate designs depicted on the vamps of the moccasins.

"Floral beadwork, just like yours," he said softly, processing the design. "They're Anishinaabe."

"Of course. Nothing but the best." Bugz smiled as Feng jumped down and sidled up next to her, wrapping his arm around her. She leaned her cheek on his shoulder as he continued to study the design of the shoes.

Feng inhaled deeply and let the life-giving breath out slowly. "What's it for?" he asked.

A truck drove by behind them as Bugz took her time responding. "It's for the children who never came home." The truck's path along the gravel road quieted slowly until Feng could barely discern it from the sound of distant insects and animals. "Remember how I told you about the residential boarding schools my grandparents and other Anishinaabe people were taken to?"

Feng nodded.

"Well, thousands of those children never came home from institutions like those across North America."

"What?"

"Yeah."

Feng's brain spun into overdrive.

"One of those institutions used to be located right here on these grounds. I remember when I was a kid, they searched the land behind the building. It was a big deal. Ceremonies—"

"Like, searched for burial sites?"

Bugz nodded, biting her lower lip. "They found some—they found some of the children. There's a plaque here listing all the names we know, and the ones we don't."

Feng followed Bugz's pointing lips, an Anishinaabe gesture he'd learned to decipher in his time on the Rez, and found a bronze plaque located a short distance away. He ran to it and sent his fingers searching down the list of names, reading out random ones, more to himself than to Bugz.

"Louis Callsforth . . . Mary Minoweya . . . unknown boy . . . unknown boy . . . unknown girl . . . " Horror crept through his heart in a way that he knew was also visible across his face. He looked to Bugz, searching her face for an explanation.

"I know, it's awful," Bugz said. "Our community built this monument to honor the children who never came home. I can't imagine anything like this. But it happ—"

"I can . . ."

Feng knew Bugz understood what he meant. He clenched his jaw tightly as he felt something stirring inside. He was overwhelmed with memories of the camp he'd been taken to as a boy in Xinjiang. The headman. The lies he'd been told about his people, lies that had made him ashamed to be Uyghur. The lies he'd been told about his family, that he'd been disowned by his parents. The pain of being separated from them. To that day he didn't even know if they were still alive. Feng felt the tears forming long before they appeared. It was as though he could feel his eyes pulling the water from throughout his body and offering it for the world to see.

He found his voice. "How many?"

"Like, in total? I don't know . . . I don't remember. But it's more than fifteen thousand."

Feng scowled. "Fifteen thousand?" He pulled his fingers from the surface of the bronze plaque and slowly walked down the pathway, stopping close to the gravel that marked the end of the walking path and the start of the road. He stared off into the distance. Feng heard Bugz's soft footsteps on the asphalt behind him.

"It's pretty awful, ain't it?"

Feng nodded. He could tell she was searching for something to say, some way to reach him, and he took a deep breath. "There was another boy back in Xinjiang that I remember. His name was Ai." Feng studied a jet stream whose brightness contrasted against the more somber tones of the clouds in the background. "We used to share a bunk bed together . . ." Feng shook his head slowly. "One day, they told me he'd been sent to the infirmary."

Feng swore at the heavens. His voice echoed slightly off the governance building behind him. He shuddered through the tears he'd long felt coming. As he worked to slow his breathing in an attempt to chase the crying away, he felt Bugz wrap her arms around him.

Feng closed his eyes and returned her hug.

CHAPTER 10

The next day, Stormy held her phone up to Bugz, who shrugged at the image displayed on the transparent screen. Bugz studied Stormy's slender fingers through the glass display, registering Stormy's messy bedroom floor that was visible behind the device. For a split second, she wondered if her own fingers looked chubby in comparison. Bugz snapped back to the moment. "I don't care what people say about me in the comment section."

"I know, I know, but this one is different. I know you're not going to like it, but it's from someone here on the Rez and it's getting lots of reactions," Stormy said.

"Alright, fine, what is it?"

"Here, it's the top comment on this video." Stormy showed her the archived livestream of Bugz dancing in plain clothes at the recent pow-wow on the Rez. Stormy tapped to open the comments and moved the phone closer to Bugz so she could read the text.

Bugz recognized the username and profile pic as belonging to someone she absolutely detested. She'd nicknamed this woman, who was her mom's age, "the traitor." This person tried to show off her supposed knowledge of Anishinaabe teachings by lecturing all the other women at a Sweat Lodge ceremony about the rules supposedly governing Anishinaabe women, mandating that they wear long skirts and otherwise occupy a position subservient to men. Bugz could already feel her blood boiling as she recalled the traitor's self-righteous and self-defeating scoldings. Not only had the traitor singled her out and shamed her, she'd done it right at the very moment they'd discovered Waawaate was sick.

Bugz shook her head as she read the comment:

"TradishOjibKwe: Omigod, what is that Holiday girl doing dancing at a pow-wow after her brother just passed away?! Doesn't she know she's not sposed to do that while she's grieving?! Does she want to make everyone sick? That's not how we did things in the #oldways #olddays.

Kids these days!

Never mind, she's probably the one who did that to her brother anyway. Did you all know she went into a sweat when she was on her time?! No wonder he got sick. I only hope no one else at that ceremony picked up that bad medicine, that 'Onjine.' Real Neechies know what I mean. What goes around comes around. I wouldn't be surprised if she gets a crooked mouth!!"

Bugz felt a familiar queasiness in her stomach and tension in the back of her neck. It was what she felt every time she became the subject of an online controversy. She'd felt this way too many times before, usually when she'd been attacked by Clan:LESS or other sexist gamers. She couldn't stand it. It was a feeling she knew she wouldn't be able to escape for days. Typically, she'd sought refuge in the real world and just spent time on the Rez trying to take her mind off of whatever was happening online. But now someone from her own community was making her feel this way.

"It's so unfair," Bugz fumed. "The emcee even told me I should go dance. And he knows I just lost my brother. He knows the traditions. This is BS!"

Sighing loudly, Bugz glanced at the subthread and saw that the comment had generated hundreds of replies and been liked more than a thousand times. She felt the pit drop further in her stomach and the unease in her neck coil its way around her spine. This anxiety seemed to buzz like the sound she heard when she passed under high-voltage power lines. Looking away from the phone and to the messy floor, Bugz scratched the back of her head and asked Stormy what the comments said.

"Honestly, I don't want to read them to you." Stormy scrolled down her screen. "But most of them are agreeing with her. Sad. Some of them are taking it way too far. People get way too serious with this stuff."

"Culture police."

"That's right." Stormy bit her lip. Bugz knew she was studying her reaction for clues about how to respond. "For what it's worth, I don't believe that stuff she's saying. I think it's about time women get treated as equal in our culture. You did the right thing by staying in that sweat, even if you were on your time."

Bugz nodded.

"It's like you made a stand for all of us," Stormy added hopefully, her intonation rising at the end, almost as if she were asking a question.

"Did you say that in the thread?"

Stormy shook her head.

Bugz felt a pang. She wished her friend would stand up and defend her, but perhaps this was too much to ask. Being a trailblazer sure felt lonely, at least at the moment. Bugz sucked her teeth and tried to compose herself. She thought of some memes she'd saved with quotes about strength, Indigeneity, and resilience. "Well, I guess it's just a sign that she's suffering. I mean, like, who would attack someone who just lost their brother? She must've experienced some deep trauma . . . and this must be how she helps cope with that."

"I'll give her some trauma, if you want," Stormy said with a grin.

Bugz scoffed and shook her head. "I know you're just saying that, but thanks. You're a real bro." The resilience she aspired to escaped Bugz's grasp. She looked around Stormy's room and at the piles of clothing covering every conceivable surface. Several empty lemonade containers lined the edge of the dresser.

"What's with the lemonade?" Bugz asked, trying to change the subject.

"Oh?" Stormy laughed, clearly embarrassed. "I don't know, I've just been craving lemonade lately. I want the freshly squeezed kind, but this store-bought is the best I can do . . ."

Bugz's thoughts drifted away from her friend's explanation. As much as she wanted to pay attention to Stormy, Bugz couldn't banish the comment section from her thoughts. "Why did she have to compare me to bad medicine? Crooked mouth? Holeee, as if I'm going to get a twisted face, like the Elders used to talk about."

Bugz thought back to the old legends she'd heard growing up, where medicine people who walked off the righteous path would have their misdeeds come back to haunt them by contorting their smiles. The stories were meant to scare the young listener away from trying to take the positive Anishinaabe traditions and subvert them with selfishness. It was the Elders' way of teaching young people not to do traditional ceremonies for fame or profit. Bugz shook her head. What they didn't intend was for this type of scolding to be used to chase someone away from pursuing their own personal healing. Bugz was sure of it.

Stormy hugged her.

Bugz nodded. "I think I'm just going to go home. Thanks for inviting me over."

"I'm sorry."

"No, you were right. It's better I know." She shook her head as she headed for the door. "Thanks."

Bugz left Stormy's house on autopilot and walked most of the gravel road home without paying attention to anything, save for the two vehicles that passed her. As each driver passed, waving as they did, Bugz couldn't shake the feeling they were thinking about the comment section and judging her for the allegations it contained. She was bad medicine. She certainly felt like it. Bugz entered her house without fanfare and ignored her mom in the kitchen as she trudged to her room.

Bugz withdrew her phone from her hoodie and saw a message in her inbox. She recognized the name of a boy a few years older than her. She opened it. "What are you thinking, Bugz? Doing all that? People like you make traditional people like me look bad!"

Bugz felt a frustration she'd known ever since she became active online begin to bubble over inside. This was the feeling that had led her to have unhealthy thoughts. She opened a window on her phone that showed her 'Versona. It looked exactly as she did at the moment, right down to the black hoodie she had on. Bugz scrunched her face. She felt disgusted at what she saw. She quickly pinched two fingers around her waist. Her 'Versona responded and its waist became smaller. A few other swipes and pinches and she'd made her online skin look more like it had in the past. More like it had when she'd been so much more popular, she thought to herself. More like what Bugz thought of as the way a beautiful Anishinaabe woman was supposed look, or at least the way she'd seen portrayed online. Less like she did in the real world.

Bugz scowled and threw her phone on the ground before falling backward on her bed. She lay on her back on the Pendleton blanket she and Waawaate used to snuggle under when they watched movies. She remembered she'd been wearing the same hoodie at her brother's funeral and thought of the giveaway.

Bugz reached into the hoodie's large front pocket and withdrew the small Dreamcatcher that she'd saved from being lost to her forever. She studied the willow hoop that fit within the palm of her hand. It looked so much more intricate and beautiful than the Dreamcatchers she saw for sale in stores or at pow-wows. This one had been made by their grandmother—the red and blue thread that formed a spider's web inside the hoop was woven in ideal geometric proportions. The pattern of the web spiraled in a concentric circle inward from the rim and wound itself in a seemingly perfect ratio along its other axis as it approached the center. Her grandmother had given it to Waawaate when he'd been having bad dreams as a child. The nightmares would get caught up in the spider's web and never reach him in his sleep, Grandma had said.

Bugz wondered whether the Dreamcatcher was still full of Waawaate's nightmares. Or perhaps everything that was happening to Bugz at that moment was the real nightmare, soon to be trapped in the well-worn web and safely transported to some place where it would never bother anyone again.

Bugz stood on her bed and hung the Dreamcatcher from the light in the center of her ceiling. She lay back on her bed, closed her eyes, and began to dream.

CHAPTER 11

Waawaate, the real Waawaate, walked along a starry path in a place that he knew was neither the real world nor the Floraverse. He looked down and saw a rattle in his left hand and a birchbark basket in his right. A knife he didn't recognize was tucked into his belt. He felt neither urgency nor impatience. Everything around him seemed very still. He stopped walking and pondered the total silence.

After a moment, Waawaate realized the pain in his hip that had haunted him for the better part of three years had disappeared. Long ago, he'd resigned himself to the fact that this pain, his cancer, would be a fellow traveler joining him on his life's journey. He'd grown accustomed to carrying it as his burden. But apparently that sense of resignation had been a mistake. He felt lighter for having left it behind.

Waawaate stepped forward, heard the soft tapping of his footsteps, and noted the beautiful moccasins that adorned his feet. He'd not seen them before. They weren't from his pow-wow regalia. Instead, they featured the pointed toes that characterized the old-style of Anishinaabe moccasins that had been worn in pre-Rez times.

Waawaate looked ahead through the Milky Way that hung all around him like a thin fog and saw someone standing on the side of the starry road in front of him. The figure was draped in shadows and its outline was traced by a beautiful shining constellation that he'd never seen before. He drew a deep breath. Just as quickly as he noticed that he could breathe freely and no longer labored to do so, the thought disappeared from his mind. The figure turned quickly and revealed herself to him.

Pulling up a black veil, and wearing a wedding dress the color of the midnight sky, there stood Stormy. She smiled sweetly and wiped her eye. She held in her hands a black bouquet. Roses the color of charcoal. The billowing black train extended behind her dress into the expanse of the universe, and it made her all the more stunning.

Has Stormy always been this beautiful? Waawaate asked himself. A dew welled in her eyes, capturing light from across the galaxy. There seemed to be nothing between them, not even air—he could see her so clearly. Her features looked soft and perfect in the brilliance of the space they inhabited. She looked to the black flowers in her hand and blinked slowly. Waawaate studied her long, dark eyelashes.

"I've missed you so much," she said slowly, raising her gaze to meet his. As their eyes locked, Waawaate lost himself to her. Stormy's smile broadened as the words echoed in Waawaate's mind. She spoke. "I want you to stay here with me."

Waawaate's heart swelled in his chest. It barely left room for him to draw a breath. Stormy had always been the prettiest girl he'd known. They'd always had a playful friendship that resolved itself into tender moments from time to time. And throughout his sickness she'd been there for him, as devoted as any soulmate would've been. She'd visited him in the hospital every single day. They'd even shared some special moments the last few times he'd been home. He'd always loved Stormy. This much was clear to him now. She loved him too, and it should be this way forever. He understood this now. Waawaate wondered why it had taken him so long to see this, and why he hadn't acted on it sooner.

Stormy held out her hand, elegant with black nail polish and black lace framing her brown skin. "I want us to be together. For eternity. Here." She turned her hand over and reached for Waawaate. "Stay with me."

Waawaate felt himself falling in love over and over again, a million times over in the span of an instant. He moved to place the birchbark basket in his pocket so that he'd be free to take Stormy's hand and embrace her here in this eternity.

As Waawaate's hand found his pocket, he felt a pouch of tobacco; suddenly, the voice of an Afro-Indigenous Elder he knew from back home entered his mind. "That isn't her," the raspy voice, wizened with age, muttered. In the vacuum of space, it was as clear as day.

Waawaate shook his head, his eyes widening. He withdrew a pinch of tobacco from the pouch, and placed it at Stormy's feet.

Quickly, as though he'd made the biggest mistake he'd ever known and was ashamed of it, he hurried down the starry path. He made sure not to make eye contact with the being he took to be Stormy as he passed by.

After he'd shuffled along some twenty steps, staring only at the stars beneath his feet, Waawaate stopped and looked over his shoulder to the one he'd thought was Stormy.

The ghastly image of a decaying corpse in a black dress stood in the spot where he'd fallen in love. Before Waawaate's eyes could widen at the terrible sight they beheld, the corpse bride screamed, lunging toward him and shattering his eardrums. The piercing cries echoed closer and closer, louder and louder, forcing him to cringe at their terrifying pitch.

Chastened, Waawaate turned forward again to face the journey ahead. His heart ached, not only for what he'd just seen, but for the real Stormy he'd known before.

CHAPTER 12

Alpha landed on the ground with a thud and cushioned the impact by crouching into a kneeling position. As he rose to his full eight-foot height, he scanned the terrain that surrounded him in the 'Verse—the rocky shores of Lake of the Torches lit by a beautiful sunny day.

Already, Bugz had him in her sights from the shadows of the forest. She could see her crosshairs shaking gently back and forth across the scar that ran the length of Alpha's face. The target moved in time with her breaths in and out. She watched him move toward the lake in a slight crouch, as though he might evade detection. He waved for his army of paratroopers, who were landing on the shores by the dozen now, to follow. He punctuated his orders to them with sexist and racist language that reminded Bugz why she detested him so much. Alpha had been the only rival to ever threaten her dominance in this domain. And now, as word had begun to spread online that Bugz was reeling from the loss of her brother and that a freak rock collapse had apparently destroyed the nest that was the source of her power, Alpha and his clanmates had decided to strike.

"Typical bully. Only picks a fight when he thinks his opponent is weak," Bugz said to Feng and the Waawaate-bot, with her eye still focused through the scope on her laser rifle. They lay next to each other in the low brush just inside the tree line. It was clear from the movements of the Clan:LESS soldiers, who turned their backs many times to the sniper rifle, that they had no idea where the trio was hiding. "Well, I suppose it's not very sporting of me to take Alpha out before he even has a chance to see us."

In her heyday as the world's top gamer, a comment like this would've struck a nerve with the followers watching her livestream and led them to shower her with tons of virtual gifts and crypto. But she hadn't felt like streaming much as she helped Waawaate through the final stages of his fight with cancer. And now that she had the Waawaate-bot to spend time with online, she hadn't been interested in starting the livestreams again. But whether she'd prepared for it or not, the moment she'd known was coming and had felt so much anxiety about had arrived—a rematch with Clan:LESS. She only hoped that her new creation could help keep the balance in her favor.

Bugz stood in the darkness, brushed the wet moss and pine needles from her black bodysuit, and stepped out into the daylight and onto the pebble beach.

"Hey, losers," she shouted. "I'm over here!"

Feng spoke to her over their voice-com. "I'm watching Alpha's stream. The chat is going nuts. They remember that's what you said before the first time you owned them . . . and now the viewers are saying you'll probably do it again." A sly grin spread across Bugz's face as she stepped farther forward. Feng's voice filled her ears again. "Dude's getting trolled on his own stream!"

Bugz kept walking forward at a nonchalant pace, extending her arms slightly and turning out her hands as though she were an angel dressed in sleek black battle gear. The neon-pink and Day-Glo-green floral designs that ran up and down her limbs shimmered in the sunshine. She heard the curses muttered from the hundreds of soldiers she'd pinned against the shore. They were furiously arranging themselves into a phalanx of cloaking shields and a secondary row of gunners. As Bugz reached the halfway point between the forest and the lake, she heard Alpha shout.

"I don't know what you're thinking, Bugz. Stop right there!" She judged the panic in his voice and scoffed. It seemed ridiculous that he might actually believe she'd obey his command. "We know you don't have any of your supernatural monsters to save you. No Thunderbirds, no diamondbacks, no underwater lizard-cat." The anxiety in his voice was unmistakable. She decided to play along, stopping momentarily.

"That's okay," Bugz replied calmly. The sly grin on her face turned into a full-on smile. "I've got everything I need right here."

On cue, Feng and the Waawaate-bot emerged from the shadows and flanked Bugz on either side, weapons drawn. They walked deliberately forward, laser guns trained on the first row of Clan:LESS warriors.

"C'mon Bugz, there's no way. Just three of you?" Alpha shouted. "This is a total mismatch."

Bugz looked to the Waawaate-bot and seemed to consider Alpha's statement. "He's right." She looked to Feng. "It is a total mismatch. Throw your weapons down, boys." She turned forward again with a look of satisfaction as she threw her laser gun into the sand at her feet. The Waawaate-bot followed suit and stood up straight, punching his fist into his open palm.

Feng, clearing his throat, spoke up. "Is it okay if I keep my weapon?"

Bugz smirked, caught off guard by Feng's interjection. "Yeah, sure." She shook her head and looked to the ground. "You kind of killed the vibe, Feng. But sure, keep your weapon."

Alpha had apparently had enough. "FIRE!" he shouted, immediately diving behind the cloaking shields for cover. A barrage of lasers, bullets, and lightning bolts came flying out of the barrels of the Clan:LESS artillery, the vast majority of them targeting Bugz, but with enough trained on Feng and the Waawaate-bot to eliminate them from the 'Verse instantly if they found their targets.

As the rain of fire closed in on the trio, time slowed to a crawl for Bugz. She jumped into a standing backflip and withdrew an infinity war club from behind her back. The weapon resembled the clubs Anishinaabe warriors used to fashion in traditional times from the knot of their chosen tree—the hardest part of the wood forming a ball at the end of a wooden handle. However, this club had been supercharged by Bugz so that it sparked with energy, like a lightning bolt in her hands. She landed on the ground in a kneeling position, and slammed the infinity war club into the rocks beneath her. The shockwave sent the pebble beach cascading toward the clanmates in a giant wave that was taller than any of them. As time returned to its normal pace, at least in Bugz's perception of it, her mastery of the stone-beings produced devastating results. The pebble tsunami deflected all of the gunfire in one instant and ran beneath the hundreds of Clan:LESS soldiers in the next, pitching them in countless directions and shattering their defenses. Bugz's powers had grown exponentially since their last major battle. The process of creating the Waawaate-bot had been a challenging journey that had forced her to tap into every skill she had in the 'Verse and to sharpen them further. She was a superhero now, bending the 'Verse completely to her will.

The Waawaate-bot would not be left behind. Immediately he replicated her feat—backflipping, slamming his own infinity war club into the earth, a new wave of rocks propelled toward the clanmates. This caused further chaos among Alpha's still-discombobulated legion of warriors. Enough of them landed on top of each other that dozens of gamertags floated up into the sky, signaling their virtual demise.

"MxNxXx has been eliminated by Bugz."

"LastYearNextYear987 has been eliminated by Bugz."

"12WpgzFinest21 has been eliminated by Waawaate-iban."

The clan quickly scrambled to return fire, though now instead of presenting a united front they splintered into groups of gunners and shield-holders each trying to fire on Bugz and her two helpers. Alpha, though caught off guard, was not one to go down lightly. He summoned the aircraft that had dropped them off to return and directed them to fly kamikaze missions at Bugz.

"The choppers are coming back at you!" Feng shouted to Bugz, his heads-up display still broadcasting a window with Alpha's livestream. "He told his pilots to sacrifice themselves for Clan:LESS."

"So dramatic," Bugz said to the Waawaate-bot, who had just Superman-punched a cloaking shield, cracking it in the process and sending the gamertags of the four clanmates hiding behind it rising to the heavens.

The first helicopter launched a volley of missiles at

Bugz from close range. She jumped into a spinning flip that she'd seen in a gymnastics documentary once, landed on the ground for a fraction of a second, and, as the helicopter blades approached, slowed time down once again. As she flipped over the crashing helicopter, Bugz planted her hand in the middle of the spinning rotors, smashed her war club through the cockpit window, and then pushed herself up into another spinning backflip toward the next helicopter beyond it. She repeated the trick again and again, destabilizing each of the helicopters she touched in the process and sending them crashing into the beach below. Finally, she smashed the window of the last chopper in this group, pushed off its rotor and, after she tucked her war club away on her back, arced into a swan dive which saw her plunge dramatically into Lake of the Torches.

When she resurfaced, treading water, she studied the shore. The Waawaate-bot had taken over in leading the destruction of the Clan:LESS army, which was down to about half its original numbers. From the clear, cool-looking waters, Bugz watched as the bot spun, flipped, and struck the clanmates who continued to fire on him mercilessly. As intent as they were on destroying him, they were no match—the Waawaate-bot was too fast and too precise. He laid waste to one soldier after another. When the occasional warrior managed to catch the bot with his back turned, Feng would pick off that member of Clan:LESS from a safe distance.

A giant, muscular Clan:LESS soldier who Bugz recognized as Feng's friend the Behemoth screamed amid the melee, "Boss! We've gotta get outta here!"

Alpha scanned his decimated forces with a nod and gave the signal to retreat over the Clan:LESS voice-com. None of the orcs, centurions, or mercenaries still on the battlefield protested. In fact, they tripped over one another as they raced up and over the still-undulating shoreline and scrambled aboard the remaining helicopters. The chopper pilots themselves were antsy to leave, and they began lifting off while their clanmates were still climbing up the dangling ropes like spiders on a waterspout.

The Waawaate-bot flew up into in a wide horizontal arc and crashed into one of the departing helicopters like a missile, dragging it to earth. Still treading water out in the lake, Bugz watched in slow motion as the bot threw those riding aboard the chopper out the open doors as it crashed to the shore below. She screamed. "Hey! That's enough! Let them retreat!"

At this, the bot turned his head toward her quizzically in the instant before the aircraft landed with a booming explosion. Bugz swam furiously to shore and then sprinted to the crash site, where she found the AI standing amidst the pile of wreckage and rising gamer-tags with a confused expression on his face. "But why?" he asked.

"Because I said that's enough. Eliminating them as they retreat is taking it too far."

The bot looked to the helicopters shrinking in the sky in a way that made it clear he was calculating whether he should obey Bugz or bolt off and destroy them.

"Look at me," Bugz said.

The Waawaate-bot returned her gaze, but lowered his head so that he was looking at her from under his brow in a way that shot a wave of tension up her back.

Bugz shook off the worry and reminded herself that she still had to teach this bot how to behave properly. "We have to carry ourselves with respect for our opponents," she explained. "After all, it's just a game. Let them come back and fight another day."

"Just a 'game'?" the bot asked, a smile lifting the corners of his mouth. "If there is something more than just this game, then let's go to whatever's outside of it and finish the job."

"No." Bugz knew she sounded frustrated, like she was speaking to a tempestuous child. "That's enough for now. Let's go do something positive. Something fun." As she said this, she realized she sounded as though she was not having any fun at all.

Bugz turned to Feng, who now stood beside her. The couple started off for the forest, leaving the AI behind. Over Bugz's shoulder, the smile slowly slipped from the Waawaate-bot's face. It disappeared from his eyes first, leaving them with a smoldering intensity. Next, the grin slid from his jaw and cheekbones, though not completely. To one side, a grimace remained, one that curled up and to the left, contorting the once-handsome face into a twisted scowl.

As Bugz took a quick glance over her shoulder to check on the bot, the smile shot back across the virtual one's face instantly, though his eyes remained ablaze. When Bugz turned to face forward again, the grin disappeared completely, leaving only a crooked mouth behind.

CHAPTER 13

Flush with nerves but still riding high from going to war alongside his girlfriend in the 'Verse the day prior, Feng knocked on the screen door. He took a step back onto Bugz's front porch. Shading his eyes from the sun with his hand, he turned to check for encouragement from his aunt Liumei, who stood a few painted wooden steps below him. Feng felt nervous, as he always did when approaching a social gathering. But this was more than just any party . . . it was a big one—Easter dinner. And to top it off, this was his first time coming to a big gathering of Bugz's family since the two of them had started dating. His anxiety racing, Feng's thoughts turned to the Waawaate-bot for some reason. There was something unnerving about the AI. Or was Feng just jealous of all the time Bugz devoted to the bot? His mind buzzed with these insecurities so intently that he considered calling the whole thing off and telling Liumei they should just go home. Just as he was about to say something to his aunt, he heard the voice of Bugz's father, Frank, boom out. "Come in!"

Bugz emerged from the basement smiling and met Feng and Liumei near the entryway. "Keep your shoes on, everyone's in the back." Feng felt some of his nerves settle as Bugz led him and his aunt through the kitchen, where Bugz's dad smiled as he tended to a foil-covered turkey. The food smelled good—so good that Feng suddenly realized he was very hungry.

As they walked out the back door and were blinded by the brilliant sunlight, the nerves hit Feng again. Bugz's entire extended family must've been here—there were close to fifty Anishinaabe people sitting in lawn chairs, on coolers, and on top of logs made to stand on their ends as makeshift stools. The people chatted and visited, covering a large expanse of the grass that led to the tree line farther behind Bugz's house. Feng looked to his feet. His aunt walked past him, offered a bowl of some kind of salad to Bugz's mom, Summer, and launched into conversation with her.

"Hey, guys." Stormy waved from a folding table where she sat playing cards with a group of Elders, each seated in a walker and eyeing Feng seriously.

"C'mon," Bugz said.

Feng looked from side to side as though there might be some way to escape engaging with the intimidating-looking old-timers. Before he could react or formulate a plan, he found himself being dragged forward by Bugz.

"Hey, everybody," he heard Bugz say as he continued to study his sneakers. "This is my friend Feng."

"Your friend," one old man with a worn baseball hat repeated with a grin.

"Just your friend?" the woman to his left asked with a knowing look as she rearranged the cards in her hand.

"Yeah," Bugz said, with a bashful smile. "And we're kind of dating, too." She paused and stood up a little straighter, apparently rediscovering her confidence. "But don't worry, we're not cousins." The table laughed at this. Feng was grateful that Bugz was in her natural element here and could help him through his nervousness. His face relaxed into a smile as she went on. "I'm practically positive we're not related. He's from China."

"China?" the Elder with the cap asked before nodding. "I visited Taiwan when I was in the military."

"Cool," Feng said quietly. He felt the eyes around the table sizing him up. He had to say something. "Actually, I'm Uyghur." More judging looks. "We're the Indigenous people of a part of China called Xinjiang."

"Oh, so you're just like us," said another woman with a full head of gray hair. "No wonder you look like you're from two Rezzes over." Feng felt himself blushing, but also somehow reassured that these Anishinaabe Elders took him almost as one of their own.

"Maybe they *are* related," the man with the hat said, sticking his tongue out as he fell into a hard laugh with the others and slammed a winning hand—a three of a kind—down on the table.

"Sit down and stay a while. Bugz, grab your boyfriend here a chair," the man said. As Bugz obliged and pulled a log over for Feng to sit on, the Elder continued. "Yeah, stick around. I want to take some of your boyfriend's money. You know how to play Texas Hold'em?"

A couple of hands later, Bugz's father emerged from the house with the turkey on a cutting board.

"Alright, circle up, folks. We're going to pray on this food and then we can eat."

"If you cooked it, we're going to need more than prayers . . . we're going to need the ambulance!" The Elder with the ball cap spoke loudly enough for everyone to hear. He turned to wink at Feng as the crowd giggled at his joke.

"Very funny, Uncle," Bugz's dad replied with a smile. "Just for that, we're going to give you the tobacco and ask you to pray for our meal." He held out a pouch of tobacco and gestured to the man with the sense of humor.

"Alright, help me up, Buggy. You too, Poker-star," the old man said. Bugz and Feng stood and gently helped the Elder to stand. As he shuffled toward the head table, they each kept a hand under his arm, more for the pageantry of it than anything else, as this old-timer was clearly able to make the trek on his own. As he arrived at the table, the sun seemed to fall just enough in the sky to turn from brilliant midday light to the golden rays that characterized the coming of dusk. The Elder spoke again. "Alright, Buggy. You and your boyfriend make a spirit dish."

Bugz stepped forward and grabbed a paper plate. "Dish out a little bit of each type of food onto this," she said softly to Feng. "We're going to offer this to the spirits."

When they completed their task, a hush fell over the crowd, and the Elder placed the tobacco pouch on top of the spirit plate. He cleared his throat and removed his hat, holding it at his side. Even the birds sang more subdued songs as he began his invocation. "Ahow kaa'anishinaa ndinawemaaganiidog. Niiyogiizhik indigo. Pizhiw gosha ndoodem."

"His name is Four Skies and he is a member of the Lynx Clan." Bugz whispered a translation to Feng. She continued on for the entirety of the man's prayer in the Anishinaabe language. He paused for a second and then spoke again in English.

"Relatives, I want to give thanks as our ancestors have for a thousand generations." He nodded his balding head and scanned the faces of those in attendance. "The springtime is the time of rebirth, of coming back to life. Of maple syrup running, suckers spawning, and the shoots of green starting to return to the trees, swamps, and shorelines.

"The Creator gave us this way of life and so we feast it every season. We do our best to line it up with the holidays. And I don't just mean these Holidays," he said, gesturing with a grin to Bugz's mom and dad, who embraced each other with a smile. "Christmas, Easter, the national holiday, and, of course, Thanksgiving line up almost exactly with the four times a year we are asked to feast our spiritual gifts. And so we do what we can to keep that alive, while making do with this world in which we are living today."

Feng scanned the faces of the Anishinaabeg who surrounded him and saw many nodding slowly, hanging on the Elder's every word.

"Creator. We say a special prayer today for this host family. They've been through so much lately, losing their son, their brother, *our* Waawaate," he said with emphasis. "We all loved that boy so much." The Elder's gaze found a point far in the distance as his eyes squinted. Feng felt Bugz reach for his hand. He squeezed back in affirmation. Four Skies spoke again. "Frank, Summer, Buggy . . ." The Elder studied each of their faces in turn. "We love you and we support you. Thank you for the food."

"Also"—the man shot a look at Feng and then smiled at Liumei—"we want to greet our new friends with a warm and hearty handshake. Welcome to Anishinaabe Akiing. Welcome to our territory. We are happy you are here with us. To be good friends. Ahow Wiisinidaa! Let's eat!"

At this, the young adults rose and began fixing plates, which they delivered to the Elders in attendance.

"Yes, we are going to be friends," Four Skies said to Feng as they returned to the card table. He then spoke in a whisper only Feng could hear. "And maybe relatives too some day?" He winked at Feng. Before Feng could respond, the Elder was on him again at full volume and with a smile on his face. "Now go get me a plate!"

After the laughs, visiting, and dessert had concluded, Bugz and Feng walked around the backyard with a garbage bag, clearing the tables. They made a few extra plates, wrapped them in foil, and distributed them to Bugz's relatives who wanted to take leftovers home. Finally, as the sun moved toward the golden hour, they completed their tasks . . . save for one.

"Take that spirit plate out to the bush, Buggy," Feng heard Bugz's father say. "After that, why don't you take him out on the boat for a bit?"

Feng nodded along with Bugz and the pair set out down a bush trail.

CHAPTER 14

Bugz was still folding the empty paper plate as they reached the dock. She looked out onto the sparkling waters of the lake around which her Rez was seated. It was named Sturgeon Lake for the extinct-in-these-parts underwater giants that had once been a staple of the Anishinaabe diet.

Bugz leapt up on the graying wooden dock and headed for the boat she'd learned to drive as a young girl. She undid the knot with one fluid motion and held the metal boat at the end of its rope.

"Don't worry, I won't push you in," Bugz said, smiling.

"Thanks," Feng replied sarcastically.

Bugz held up the crossed fingers she'd been hiding behind her back. "Just kidding," she said, still with a smile on her face. Once Feng was on board, Bugz pushed off from the dock, slid onto the bow of the boat, and quickly made her way past Feng to the stern. As the boat spun slowly to face deeper water, Bugz pumped the primer bulb until her hand was sore, turned the key, and heard the motor fire. She worked the throttle and the boat sprang forward. The humming motor drowned out all other sounds. Bugz glanced back to inspect the healthy wake the boat left in its trail and then looked forward again.

The lake opened up before her, dark blue waves expanding toward the horizon, framed by treed islands on either side. Somehow, Bugz felt as though her field of view was much broader than it had been just a few moments ago. There was seemingly so much more sky and even more water all around her. Her spirit soared above it all. *Damn,* she thought to herself, *I forgot what it's like to be out here.* She told herself it was almost like being on Lake of the Torches in the 'Verse. She thought of Waawaate.

"How are you doing?" she yelled to Feng.

He gave a thumbs-up.

"Don't worry, we're not going too far," Bugz shouted over the motor. She steered the boat in a wide bank around a set of islands and turned the throttle again, checking to make sure they were at top speed. The lake spit the odd drop of water on her as the waves sped by. The remaining sun bounced brilliantly off their crests. Bugz breathed the fresh air in deeply.

After making her way around a few other islands, and making enough turns to completely disorient Feng, Bugz headed into a channel that ran between two large islands. As they approached the midway point, the islands seemed to rise higher into the sky. The treetops above each hill blocked out so much light it felt as though the sun was disappearing much more quickly from the sky. Bugz throttled down and the boat slowed to a near stop. As she turned the key to the off position, the boat rocked gently as waves from the wake bounced off the shoreline and made their way back to them. Silence spread across the water. Bugz breathed deeply again and radiated a look of utter contentment. She soaked up the lapping waves and turned the rudder to spin the boat slightly in the channel so that its bow now faced one of the shores.

"There it is," Bugz said to Feng, who scanned his surroundings. It was clear he hadn't expected to be looking for anything. "Up there, behind those trees on the giant rock face." Bugz gestured with her chin and pointed to the cliff slightly with her lips.

Only the small waves tapping softly against the boat punctured the silence. Bugz looked to the far end of the channel and saw sunlight still shining on the waters past the island's most distant shore. She looked back to the rock.

"It's a rock painting. A really big one. Do you see it?" she asked.

"Oh, yeah!" Feng answered, with a genuine surprise in his voice as he recognized the huge ocher forms that colored the gray cliff. "That thing must be fifty feet long."

He squinted as he tried to decipher it. "What is it? An arrow or something?"

Bugz smiled. "No, you're looking at it backwards. Our people recorded and drew things from right to left, to mirror the sun traveling from east to west. So the parts you think are the arrow's fletching on the left are actually new roads and possibilities shooting off and opening up from the right." Bugz dipped a paddle into the water and maneuvered them closer to the shore.

"It's the Everlasting Road—Gaagigewekinaa," she said, looking to her feet. "That's the path you walk on through life." She sighed almost imperceptibly. "And that's the path that souls take after they leave this world . . ."

Bugz moved past Feng, grabbed a rope from the bow of the boat, and jumped to the shore. She pulled the boat up onto the rocks, tied a knot around a nearby tree, and returned to offer her hand to Feng. With her help, he managed to jump down onto dry land.

"Ladies first," Bugz said, pushing by Feng with a smile and arch of her eyebrows. "C'mon. Let's go take a look."

A short climb later, they stood in front of the archetypal masterpiece. Though the painting was clearly weathered, the rust-colored strokes seemed to have been indelibly imprinted onto the rock. The centerline that traveled from east to west was as thick as Bugz's forearm was long. She held her arm up to compare. Every five steps or so a diagonal line jutted off up toward the western sky or down toward the western earth. Bugz led Feng along the length of the rock painting.

"The Elder who prayed for us, Four Skies, he brought us here as kids and taught us what this means."

"The Everlasting Road."

"Yeah." She ran her fingers along the rock face beneath the art. "Each of these diagonal lines is a different path your life can take. You can go off into these random directions. Get into trouble. Do things that aren't healthy. Whatever." She touched the centerline and a speck of paint flecked off. She withdrew her hand with a start. "It's up to us to stay true. To keep moving forward on the path that we're supposed to." Bugz nodded her head slightly.

"That's powerful," Feng replied. He drew a deep breath and nodded in appreciation. "Your people really had a lot figured out."

Bugz felt her heart grow a little heavier. "They say the same is true of the afterlife. As you journey to the Happy Hunting Grounds, there are many trials, tribulations, and distractions along the way. You have to stay true and keep moving forward to get to that place where we can all be together again . . ." Bugz looked to the sky, which she noticed was now a gradient of royal and deep navy blues. The day was growing late. "Someday."

Bugz looked back to Feng. He stepped forward and reached for her arms in a gentle hug. She leaned in and gave him a quick embrace before pulling away just as fast. Bugz felt she was short-changing Feng again, but she also felt powerless to stop it. Bugz could recognize the romantic potential in the majestic setting and the fact they were alone. But all she felt in her heart was loneliness. She missed Waawaate so much.

Bugz retrieved a small pouch of tobacco from her pocket that she'd kept from the spirit dish. "We should make an offering to honor this teaching," she said. "And to honor the Ancestors who left this for us."

Bugz placed the tobacco at the foot of the rock face, closed her eyes, and whispered a prayer of grateful words. As she finished, her heart remained unfulfilled.

CHAPTER 15

Feng chipped away at the virtual rock face delicately and carefully . . . at least as carefully as he could with a hammer. Further complicating things was the fact he was dangling hundreds of feet above the ground by a mountain-climbing rope he'd rappelled down the side of the cliff with. *Heights don't bother me in the Floraverse*, he lied to himself. Though the scene was virtual, when he stopped hammering and blew powdered rock fragments away from the site of his handiwork, he felt his entire body tense as he detected a slight swing of the rope that suspended him. *No problem. I just won't blow on the rock face anymore. Or breathe.*

This had all seemed like a good idea to him when he'd decided to start work on this project after visiting the rock painting with Bugz. He'd been inspired to work with cliffs and stone, just as her ancestors had. He'd developed his plans over the following days. But now, a week later, his hands were shaking from his fear of virtual heights.

Feng opened a window in front of him that displayed computer-aided design drawings of the massive structure he was intent on building. He snapped the window shut and resumed chipping away at the rock face. He'd been at it for an hour and he was still working on his first tube. He planned to tunnel a few feet farther into the rock, deposit a stick of TNT, and then repeat that feat a few dozen times before moving a safe distance away, where he would set off the explosives and leave behind the reimagined rock face. He was motivated and determined, no matter how long it seemed to be taking. He reached back and struck the hammer especially hard, trying to clear a large granite fragment, but the recoil from his tool sent him turning slightly on the rope. When his body detected this motion, he reacted instinctively, overcorrecting and sending himself spinning in the opposite direction like a top.

The virtual world around Feng became a blur of spinning colors, half rock face and half sky. He closed his eyes and waited helplessly for his 'Versona to stop spinning.

Once it did, he took a deep breath and started chipping away at the rock face again.

"What are you doing?" A loud, unmistakable voice shocked Feng so much that he jumped in place and started spinning on the end of the rope again.

The Waawaate-bot stopped him immediately and smiled at him widely. "What are you doing up here, spinning over and over again? That's what I meant to ask."

"Never mind," Feng said, attempting to focus back on the rock face and resuming his hammering.

"Come on, tell me," the bot said from the right of Feng, who simply shook his head in reply. The bot teleported to Feng's left side and asked again. "Come on, please, man!"

"God, you're annoying."

"Why is god annoying?" the bot said, snickering.

"Get out of here, I said."

"Just tell me and I'll leave you alone," the Waawaate-bot said in a convincing tone.

"Fine," Feng said, exasperated. "I'm making a monument to the kids who never came home from the residential boarding schools."

For the first time in Feng's experience the AI was silenced. When the bot did resume speaking, he said "That's pretty cool," in an uncharacteristically thoughtful voice. He jumped back to Feng's right, resuming his energetic pace. "So you're going to turn this mountain into a monument. But it's going to take you forever to carve this giant monument with that little hammer."

Feng smiled. "I'm not going to carve it. I'm just placing dynamite. And then I'm going to blast it into the rough shape."

"Really? Cool!" A huge grin broke out across the Waawaate-bot's wide-eyed face. "You've got to let me help you."

"You said you were going to leave me alone."

"No, I can help you speed it up, I'm sure. Show me the design."

Feng sighed, recognizing the bot would be relentless with his pestering if he didn't get his way. He hung the hammer in his belt and opened a window again. He angled it toward his companion, showing a massive statue depicting rows of Anishinaabe children posed together just as Indigenous children had been forced to sit in countless historic residential boarding school photos. But in Feng's design, these seated children did not wear the identical appearances forced onto them by the institutions.

"Wow, you designed that?" the bot asked, his face wearing a studious expression.

Feng couldn't help feel a little pride at how seriously his automated companion was taking his plans. "Yes," he said, pausing to collect his thoughts. "When I was searching up the history of those institutions, I saw so many photos like this of the kids: shoulder to shoulder, all forced to look the same with their outfits, same haircuts. But you could see on their faces they weren't cookie cutter. They were each unique . . ." Feng faced an uphill battle to complete this sentence as his own institutional memories flooded his mind. He thought of the uniform he'd been made to wear in Xinjiang, like a thousand other kids at his camp. Nothing like the clothing his parents provided for him at home to wear day to day. Even further from the beautiful traditional Uyghur clothing they used to dress him in on special occasions. The memory swelled in his mind such that he had to draw a deep breath into his chest quickly. "And . . ." Feng cleared his throat.

"Beautiful." The bot completed his thought. Feng wondered if the automaton could feel empathy. He wondered if the AI could sense how much the resilience of Anishinaabe children in the residential boarding schools meant to him, reminding him of his own ability to survive and adapt as a child taken from his parents. Feng noticed his jaw had tightened.

Feng's line of thinking was interrupted by the bot, who launched into a rapid-fire series of short sentences laying out his ideas for how to execute Feng's vision faster. The bot seemed to be in a trance of sorts, spitting out his plans with the rat-a-tat rhythm of a skilled rapper or spoken-word poet. Before Feng could process most of what he'd said, the bot concluded with, "So I guess what I'm saying is, just give me the TNT and let me take it from here. Yeah, gimme the dynamite. Hand it over."

Feng was caught off guard by the demand, not least of all because there was something unsettling in how obsessed the bot had become. But he seemed committed to the same goal as Feng—to honor the children who'd never come home from those terrible institutions—and he seemed respectful of Feng's vision. As he weighed his options, Feng was forced to conclude that it would probably take him years to complete the project if he were to keep chipping away at the mountainside one hammer strike at a time. The bot could probably complete it much faster than that.

Feng reached over his shoulder and swung the backpack full of explosives over toward the bot, extending the bag as an offering. In the moment before the bot took the gift, Feng felt a flash of nerves run through his heart.

The AI snatched the bag from Feng, who was shocked at the speed with which the bot moved. Before Feng could even crane his head to look up the rock face, the Waawaate-bot had already snatched the hammer from his belt, scurried up the climbing rope, and jumped to three separate spots on the side of the cliff. In each of these locations, and in only a blink of an eye, the AI had carved a small tunnel and deposited a stick of dynamite inside. Soon the bot was a blur of activity, darting from side to side and up and down the mountain, drilling thousands of holes of different depths, each corresponding to some detail on the plan, and laying the explosives inside. In what felt like less time than it would have taken Feng to chug a can of soda, the Waawaate-bot was finished. He scurried quickly back down the rope toward Feng and spoke with a quizzical look on his face. "You know what?" the bot started. "I think I've got a better idea than to hang out with you here. Forgive the pun."

Before Feng could object, the Waawaate-bot had scampered back up the mountainside and began pulling the climbing rope up with the speed of a CrossFit athlete trying to finish a fitness challenge. The bot then snatched

Feng by his harness and flew to another nearby mountain, this one only about a quarter of the size of the first. He landed softly on the summit. Here, the bot and Feng had a clear view of the mountain they planned to carve with explosives.

"Hey!" Feng shouted, betraying the fear he felt. He paused and lowered his voice. "I mean . . . thanks for all your work, but could you take it a little easy? You just about sent me flying down the side of that mountain."

"Uh-huh, uh-huh, uh-huh." The bot spit these words out with the speed of a machine gun, though the smile on his face conveyed more eager child than soldier. "Definitely, I can take it easy, and I'm making a note of it right now, but do you want to hit the switch?"

"What?"

"Pull the trigger, light the fuse, blow the mountainside."

"Really? You mean it's done? Everything?"

The bot nodded as enthusiastically as a dog being asked to go for a walk. He leapt with excitement as he saw Feng begin to double-check the work done against his plans. "It's finished, just hit it!" The AI shook his head frantically.

Feng retrieved the detonator from his pocket. It was a small black device that fit in the palm of his hand and it featured only one large round button. He looked up to the giant mountain before him. The snow-capped peak gave way to that massive cliff of midnight black and blue striations framed by dark gray slopes on either side. Closer to the horizon, the lush forests first lit up the foothills in the brilliant red, amber, and ocher colors of a permanent fall before giving way to the evergreen tones of the coniferous trees above, closer to the tree line. The sun dipped just enough to lengthen the waves of virtual light so they now bathed the scene in an autumnal glow. Feng felt as though he could sense the cool, crisp air in this majestic scene. *My mind's playing tricks on me.*

Feng thought of the detention camp in Xinjiang. He thought of his tormentors in the Chinese Communist Party. He thought of the years of his childhood that he'd been deprived of spending with his parents. Feng squeezed the device in his hand.

Rocks exploded like fireworks in the distance, first from the top of the mountain. Snow and gravel shot in all directions, resembling gray and white palm trees in the sky. A rapid-fire series of explosions went off like firecrackers, their charges puncturing the heights of the mountain before running down its side toward a valley floor below. Soon, these relatively tiny explosions caused rock slides to start careening down under the force of gravity. Feng caught himself holding his breath.

Finally, three large, deep booms rocked their surroundings and rumbled through the earth beneath Feng's feet. There was a momentary calm during which Feng noticed himself breathing again. Three massive columns of rock that traced their way up the entire mountain began to give way. These huge would-be skyscrapers began to sink, collapsing on their bases as they receded into the land below. As they did, they kicked up a huge cloud of dust that rushed toward Feng and the bot.

Feng recalled a sandstorm he'd seen as a boy, back when he still lived with his parents. They'd gone out to the country together for a picnic and had been caught off guard by the howling early winds. As they'd raced home, he'd been whipped by the flying grains of silica and had buried his head in his mother's side for protection. She'd held him close amidst the swirling chaos until finally his father picked him up like a baby, wrapped him in their picnic blanket, and sprinted the rest of the way home. They'd made it just in time. They slammed the door, blocked the windows, and sheltered in place as what sounded like a terrible, humongous monster made its way overhead. Feng judged he must've been three years old at the time. This event had been buried deep in his subconscious for years, but as the virtual dust cloud overtook him, so too did this memory. As the virtual grains of sand blew by his face he imagined that he could feel them whipping his cheeks and forehead just as that sandstorm had in western China so long ago. He thought of turning to hide his face in his mother's embrace. Yet he knew that if he were to turn to find her she would not be there.

Unable to see anything in the Floraverse, save for the generic beige dust that had been kicked up in all directions, Feng sank deeper into the recesses of his mind. His parents had always protected him. *Until they couldn't.* Feng thought of the government officials who separated his family. *The one thing my parents couldn't protect me from. Everything went wrong from there. Detention. Shame. Exile. Loneliness.*

Feng's thoughts cleared with the settling dust. As the cloud gave way, a brilliant picture emerged. Three rows of twenty Indigenous children, each of them hundreds of feet tall, sat in place, shoulder to shoulder. Their hands were clasped in their laps, in much the same way as in the old residential boarding school photos.

But here is where Feng's vision took over—in this new virtual monument, the giant faces of the children radiated pure, serene happiness. Their clothing bore the traditional floral beadwork of the Anishinaabe. Their hair was long. Each wore braids in a unique design, evidently set into style by the loving, caring hands of their parents, who were no doubt raising them.

This was the image of Indigenous children as they always should have been. Proud, happy, and rooted in the full warmth and beauty of their cultures, families, and homes. The virtual sun sank deeper and cast the children in the red of the dying day.

"It's beautiful, Feng." The bot patted Feng on the back. "What a beautiful sight."

Feng wondered if the experiences of these children meant anything to the bot. He debated again whether the virtual being could feel empathy. He glanced at the AI and pondered whether this monument was only that to him—a pretty sight. He looked back to the statue.

To Feng, it meant something deeper.

CHAPTER 16

After logging out of the Floraverse, Feng stared at his blank bedroom walls and thought about the Waawaate-bot. He was grateful the bot had helped him build his monument and appreciated that the AI had made him feel good about his design. Yet part of Feng knew that there was something wrong with the AI. He'd always sensed it, right from those first moments in the underwater cavern. Perhaps it was just a simple aversion to the bot resembling someone he knew was dead, but maybe it was something more . . . some sense that the bot had the cunning of a human being but lacked something else.

Feng threw a tennis ball at the wall and caught it after a bounce. He still didn't think he could talk to Bugz about how he felt. The AI meant so much to her. Would she like Feng less if he criticized her creation?

After pondering this for a moment further, Feng walked down the hall and found his aunt Liumei sitting at the table staring at her phone.

"Hey," he offered, walking over and pulling up a chair. As he did, he noticed his aunt's serious expression. "What's up?"

"Nothing. How are you? How was school?"

Feng tried to lean into his aunt's field of view, but she refused to return his gaze. He answered her. "Fine. Same as every day . . . crowded homeroom and then empty hallways." He flashed a mischievous grin. "Except for us Rez kids."

Liumei smiled. "You've come a long way from that first car ride when I brought you here. You looked at me like moving to the Rez was literally going to kill you." She spun her phone on the table in front of her. "You still wish you'd moved to Beijing instead?"

"I dunno." Feng leaned back with a slight smile still on his face. "But may as well make the most of my time here, right? Plus, Bugz is cool."

"Yeah, I'm glad you've got a good friend in her. Girlfriend. Whatever."

With this, Liumei stood and retrieved a plate from the microwave and placed it in front of Feng. "I had a long day at work . . . so leftovers tonight, okay?"

"That's fine," Feng said, pushing the food around his plate as he blew on it. After stick-handling the day-old takeout food a moment more, he devoured it as though it were his last meal.

"You always eat like you're starving," his aunt observed. Feng smiled, chewing, but not breaking the pace at which he made the food disappear.

After Feng put his plate in the sink, he walked back to the table to pick up his phone. Just as he was about to bound off to his bedroom, his aunt asked him to sit down again. "There's something we need to talk about," she said.

"Okay, what's up?"

Liumei evaded Feng's eyes, weighing her words carefully. For a small eternity, Feng wondered whether she'd ever begin to speak.

"There's a video."

"Okay . . ."

"It's making the rounds on social media."

"Of Bugz? Yeah, she's been telling me about it. It's pretty messed up—"

"No. Not of Bugz. I mean, I'm sure there is a video of Bugz or whatever. But that's not what I'm talking about."

Liumei swiped up on her screen and found the clip in question on her phone. She angled her phone away from Feng, as though weighing one final time whether or not to show her nephew the clip. "It's a video that shows your mother and father." Liumei looked to Feng. "In China." She cleared her throat.

Feng felt as though his spirit were separating from his body, as though he were watching himself from over his own shoulder. He could see the back of his head as he sat at the dinner table with Auntie Liumei. "What? When?" he managed to force out.

"This week," his aunt offered. She placed her phone down and stared at Feng, dew in her eyes. "Feng—your parents are alive."

CHAPTER 17

The Waawaate-bot bounded from side to side behind Bugz with an enthusiastic smile on his face, practically radiating energy. As much as she enjoyed feeling like her brother was still with her here, deep in this virtual forest, Bugz was starting to find his increasingly frantic nature to be a bit much. She was trying to focus so that she might conjure up some new supernatural creatures in the Floraverse—to help them in case Clan:LESS or anyone else launched another raid. She'd been able to turn her enemies away herself when she was fully engaged with the fight, but she was less sure of what would happen if they attacked again when she wasn't logged in. The recent showdown on the shore had reminded her of the need to rebuild her defenses. But the bot kept interrupting.

"Hey, what's with the new look?" the AI asked quickly. "You look great. I think the bodysuit is cool.

Very functional. Very warrior-goddess. But why did you change it up? Why ditch the hoodie, you know?"

If the bot were trying to aggravate Bugz, he could scarcely do better than call attention to her virtual appearance. It triggered all of the insecurities she tried to bury beneath her 'Versona's skin.

"Can you chill for a second, Waawaate?" Bugz said, doing her best to sound good-natured, and forcing a smile for good measure.

"Sure, I'm chill, I'm chill, I'm chill. I don't have to ask about that," the bot replied as he began teleporting from one side of Bugz to another. "I just want to see everything you're doing so I can learn to do it too."

"That's cool, but to be honest, I can't focus on what I'm doing when I feel you watching me from every angle."

"Right." The Waawaate-bot stood still, smile still plastered across his face.

Bugz noticed the virtual birds chirping around the periphery of the clearing they stood in. She felt inspired to make a Thunderbird. In her mind's eye, she pictured the supernatural jet-black raptor. *Beautiful,* she thought. She summoned a bird from a nearby tree. As it landed on the palm of her outstretched hand, Bugz closed her eyes with a serene look on her face.

The small blackbird hopped in place and became two before it landed again on her palm. Almost instantly, those two blackbirds doubled, before doubling again, and then again. Bugz lifted her outstretched palm slowly in front of herself. The exponentially growing number of blackbirds flew in thousands of concentric flight paths around each other. It looked as though Bugz were lifting a giant, writhing black beach ball in front of her as the birds swarmed around one another, darting in and out of thousands of orbits. Bugz had done this dozens of times before. The crucial step of melding these count-less individual birds into one giant majestic beast could be executed in just a few more moments. But it required her utmost focus. She could sense the Waawaate-bot starting to fidget behind her.

Bugz clenched her eyes tighter together, now scrunching her forehead with effort. The writhing sphere of flying birds began to undulate slightly and extend at two opposite horizontal ends. The birds kept flying at extraordinary speeds around these tight flight paths as the sphere continued to flatten and began to spread wings. The Thunderbird was starting to take shape. But the bot behind Bugz was growing too excited. She could feel him teleporting to multiple locations all around her. Bugz knew that if she looked at him, he'd have that ridiculous smile on his face. She summoned her willpower to avoid opening her eyes. The final step lay just ahead.

With her free hand, Bugz reached up to the sky to conjure lightning. Clouds formed in the sky and began to swirl high above. Soon they lowered in a spiral toward her. She could practically feel the static charge building in the air above her. *Here it comes in three . . . two . . . one . . .* , Bugz thought to herself.

In her mind's eye, Bugz could picture what to do next. She would bring her free hand down quickly, clapping the other, and the lightning would strike the birds and transform them into the beautiful flying legend she craved to see again. The bot began to giggle with excitement as he continued to jump back and forth behind her.

Thunder rolled heavily and shook the ground on which they stood. The bot couldn't handle it anymore. "So cool!" he shouted without warning.

Bugz flinched and opened her eyes. As she glared at the Waawaate-bot, the blackbirds scattered into innumerable directions, disappearing into the far reaches of the Floraverse.

Bugz huffed and the clouds slunk away slowly, leaving the clearing in daylight again.

Now completely still, the Waawaate-bot wore the expression of a child who'd just dropped a plate on the floor. The upward curl on the left side of his mouth only accented the sense that he'd been busted doing something wrong. He glanced from side to side before finally offering a "sorry."

Bugz simply shook her head and sighed as she walked off down the nearest bush trail. She felt so frustrated. But she didn't want to rage at the image of her brother, the one she missed so much.

Then again, if it were the real Waawaate, I'd be fine with yelling at him. She stopped and turned around. A step behind her on the bush trail was the bot, looking from side to side as though he'd been busted again.

"Listen, that really pissed me off," Bugz said, flaring her nostrils.

"I didn't mean to—"

"Don't interrupt, you're only making it worse. I really like having you around, I really do. But unless you learn to chill, we're going to have to take some breaks from each other." Bugz felt guilty the moment she spoke the words. She'd created this being for the sole purpose of spending time with her. Now she, his maker, was telling him he was somehow failing at that task—his reason for being. She could see the confusion on the bot's face. As she studied his face, the thought popped into Bugz's mind of drawing her infinity war club and smashing it into the replica. Bugz shook her head to chase the thought away.

"Can I help you some other way? Even if we're not together?" The bot interrupted her thoughts.

"No, it's fine. Never mind."

"How about if I chase down those Clan:LESS noobs?"

"No, forget it. I'm just feeling off."

The ensuing back-and-forth completely eradicated what remained of Bugz's patience. For every explanation she offered, the Waawaate-bot came up with a rationale for why he should pursue their enemies. As the volley wore on, Bugz realized that since he was a computer simulation, her companion would never tire and could continue for much longer than she could. The thought discouraged her.

"I'm going to log off for a bit and we can talk again later," Bugz said.

"Hold on."

"What?"

"That's it. That's how I'll get them . . . I'll pursue them into the AR."

Bugz scrunched her forehead to convey her bewilderment. The augmented reality version of the 'Verse spanned the globe, but it was tied to the user's real-world location. The Spirit World, the virtual reality incarnation of the 'Verse they were currently inhabiting, was the only forum where people in different real-world locations could interact.

"That doesn't make sense. Moving from AR to the Spirit World is a one-way street. No one can follow anyone back into the AR because we're still in different real-world locations," Bugz said. "To follow them, you'd need to teleport or something."

"Ah, my virtual sister, but you forget. I have no physical location. I'm all digital. I can follow anyone anywhere I like."

Bugz processed this and instantly recoiled at the thought of this energetic, rambunctious, and unpredictable bot running free, anywhere in any domain of the Floraverse he chose, whether augmented reality or virtual. He clearly couldn't control himself. She shook her head. "I'm going to log off and we can talk about this later. Don't do anything about this until we talk again, promise?"

The Waawaate-bot nodded his head, smiling. As Bugz removed her headset, she couldn't see the AI's fingers crossed behind his back, or the contortion running up one side of his mouth as the smile disappeared from his face.

Returning to the real world, Bugz pulled the headset off and ran her hand through her hair. She still couldn't get used to how short it was now. She flipped off the light switch on her bedroom wall and studied the silhouette of the Dreamcatcher hanging from the fading light.

"Don't fail me now," she said to it.

CHAPTER 18

Bugz and Stormy walked through the crowded hallways of their school as the speakers blared out public health instructions. The teens had heard these so often throughout their lives that they simply faded into background noise. Bugz held her phone out in front of her, a clear glass rectangle that appeared to project the augmented reality of the Floraverse onto the world visible behind it. As she walked beside her friend, Bugz occasionally tilted and moved her phone from side to side to check out the 'Versonas of the other students walking around them. Nothing out of the ordinary. Mostly off-the-rack skins, nothing like the customized skins real gamers like her used. In spite of all the judgment she was passing on her peers, every time they passed another kid from the Rez, Bugz felt as though she were the one being judged.

"I swear, that comment from the traitor." Bugz shook her head. "I feel like everyone I know is looking at me different."

"It's all in your head, girl," Stormy answered, looking not at all convinced of her words as she checked her makeup on her own phone's screen. "Hey, I like your new look, by the way. Your 'Versona, I mean. Looking good."

Bugz felt a pang. The 'Versona that looked less like she did in real life. Or maybe Stormy was just being nice and didn't actually have a preference for Bugz's skin in the game. "Thanks" was all Bugz could muster. She heard the homeroom bell ringing.

"Sorry, Bugz. I don't know what I said, but I'm just trying to make sure I don't look like a mess. Homeroom is lights, camera, action, you know?" Stormy smiled. "Besides, even though we all know you're a superstar, the whole world doesn't revolve around you, okay lil missy?"

"Okay, I'll see you later."

Bugz rounded a hallway corner and bumped into Feng, who was rushing to make it to their homeroom. They mumbled greetings to each other and instantly Bugz could see something was bothering him. He evaded her eyes as he trudged into class and toward his desk. Bugz took her place in the desk next to his cautiously, as though she had to embody the trepidation she felt.

"What's the matter?"

"Everything."

Bugz scowled slightly. Feng wasn't prone to melodrama. As their teacher, Mr. Harbach, walked into the classroom and started to take attendance, Bugz pulled out her phone and messaged Feng. After a few back-and-forth texts, and circling around the issue at the heart of his worries, Bugz managed to draw out of Feng the existence of the video featuring his parents.

Bugz grimaced at her phone as the teacher called her out for using a device she wasn't supposed to during class. She apologized and leaned back in her chair.

In the first few months after meeting Feng, she'd learned that his relationship with his parents had caused him a lot of pain. He'd confided in her about the traumas of his childhood as they walked deep in the forest near the Rez—how he'd been taken from his family at a young age and put in a Uyghur re-education camp run by the Chinese Communist Party. Feng had shown her a video of him as a child in which a guard at the camp had said his parents chose their religion over him, their own child. It was a lie, but it was a lie Feng had believed for many years. It had only been in coming to the Rez, and after participating in ceremonies with Bugz's family, that Feng finally began to see through the lies he'd been told as a boy.

Bugz had also heard Feng say he suspected his parents were dead. As she looked over to him and saw the stern look on his face, her heart felt drawn to him, as though she wanted to protect him. She realized the video meant Feng's parents were still alive, which should've given him some hope. But he certainly didn't look hopeful. *Probably wondering why they haven't reached out,* she thought.

Feng held up his phone and waved it at Bugz without making eye contact. Bugz looked to her phone and saw he'd sent her a copy of the new video of his parents. It bore meme-like text on top promising "Shocking Uyghur Confession."

Careful not to be too obvious, Bugz placed the phone in her lap and set it to mute. With a few taps she set her automatic translator to generate captions on screen that transcribed the Mandarin into English in real time. She tapped the play button and saw two people in drab clothing. The man resembled Feng, though his windburned cheeks suggested that he worked outside. Lines around the man's eyes distinguished him as a generation older than Feng, and the thick beard gave him a sense of gravitas. The woman beside him appeared weary beyond belief and was very skinny. Yet her large, dark eyes grabbed Bugz and pulled her in. Even through this tiny screen, Bugz felt she could stare into those eyes and see the depths of the universe. It was the same way she'd felt when she'd first met Feng's gaze. Bugz paused the video and studied the woman's high cheekbones and olive skin. The woman would not have looked out of place on the Rez for her features, Bugz thought. These had to be Feng's parents. The video was timestamped with a date earlier in the week and showed a location in China in the bottom left corner of the screen. Bugz whispered the captions to herself.

"We are here, Mr. and Mrs. Turukun, to admit to the flaws of our previous ways and to swear our allegiance to the People's Republic of China and the party that serves the people so perfectly," Feng's father began. His mother picked up the script and outlined a number of her personal flaws.

They began to renounce their religion in increasingly bizarre terms until, finally, Feng's mother said, at least according to the automatic translator, "the truth is that our religion is backward and asks us to harm our own children. It's sad, but true. That's why . . ." On screen, she was overcome by tears. Feng's father looked to her quickly and then back to the camera and continued in his wife's place. "That's why it's good the party took our only son from us. To protect him from us." Feng's father looked to the ground and reached for his wife's hand.

Bugz shut the video off and pursed her lips as she tried to process what she had just seen. She looked to Feng, who stared straight at the front of the classroom. She typed a message on her phone and hit send, imploring him by text: "Ignore it! It's just propaganda." She cleared her throat, trying to get Feng's attention, but he ignored her. She texted him again: "The main thing's they're alive! You can see them again." She sniffed, though her nose was clear. Feng refused to engage. Finally, she picked up her phone a third time and heard Mr. Harbach speak from the front of the class.

"That's quite enough, Ms. Holiday. Go to the office and explain to the vice-principal why you have to text and bother Feng during homeroom."

CHAPTER 19

The Behemoth, a gargantuan rock of a warrior with twin Ø tattoos on each bicep—symbols representing his allegiance to Clan:LESS—stood atop a cliff in the Floraverse, brandishing a massive energy cannon. The Clan:LESS member was careful to strike a pose each time he shifted his position with his prized virtual possession. He was streaming to a growing number of followers who regularly showered him with gifts and crypto. It'd been enough for him to quit his day job as a barista in a city on one of the coasts thousands of miles from the Rez. The recent beatdown of the clan that was not a clan by Bugz, Feng, and the Waawaate-bot had been an unexpected boon for the Behemoth—it had created the impression among many gamers that Alpha was overrated and that the Behemoth was the true mastermind of the operation. Judging by the millions of subscribers who now followed him, he was at the very least the fan favorite.

"Pull!" the Behemoth yelled. A dozen neon-orange discs went flying into the sky above him. He fired his cannon once and the discs exploded. "One shot, six kills, bang-bang-bang-bang-bang-bang!" He continued to mug for the audience watching his stream.

"Pull, pull, pull!" he shouted, and an automated launcher fired three times as many discs into the sky above him. He dispatched them with similar ease. "And that's Target Shooting 101, folks. Get a wild weapon like this and it makes it all so easy." He blew imaginary smoke from the barrel of his cannon like a sharpshooter in the westerns of old. "Smash that subscribe button and tell your friends. I'm doing another giveaway this week. Subscribers with the most referrals will win a chance to come to the range with me and test your skills against"— he swiped his hands in the air a few times in a cheap imitation of kung-fu before continuing—"the Behemoth."

The Behemoth swiped the livestream closed and counted the gifts and micro-payments he'd received— enough to cover his expenses for the month. He smiled at his good fortune as he collapsed his projectile launcher, stuffed it into his bag, and started walking down the hill to be swallowed by the virtual forest.

"Hey, marksman," an unfamiliar voice beckoned him from the dark forest trail ahead. The Behemoth froze in his place.

"Who's that?"

"An old friend."

"Alpha? Is that you?" The Behemoth strained to see into the darkness. "I can invite you onto one of my upcoming streams if you want," he said with an uneasy tone. He worried what his boss thought of his newfound success. "Good news, sir. I've been doing really well with these streams and I've got quite a lot saved up to help us rebuild our clan." The Behemoth felt a little ashamed by how much sucking up his voice conveyed.

Silence greeted him, so he continued slowly down the trail. The forest grew darker. Everything seemed to take on a more sinister feel. The crows cawing suddenly felt like they were warning him. The silence of the virtual insects creeped him out. A twig snapped to his left. The Behemoth froze and spun quickly toward the source of the sound.

"Alpha? C'mon out, man, let me see ya." He cursed the nerves in his voice. He cleared his throat and spoke again. "I mean, it'd be good to see ya, right?"

Another footstep snapped another branch, this time closer, but still he could see nothing.

"I'm not Alpha," the voice said.

"Well, who are you then?"

The voice spoke again, but now it was directly behind him. "We've met before."

The Behemoth spun 180 degrees and could finally make out the figure in the darkness. He studied the long blue and green fringes that hung from the specter's regalia. His eyes traced their way up his pursuer's body. As his gaze rose, it found a cruelly twisted mouth that curved up to the left. The Behemoth felt his heart skip a beat. He pulled out his energy cannon and, in the split-second before he fired it, he saw the missing half of the crooked smile climb up this phantom's face to form a fully devilish grin.

As the energy fire tore through the depths of the forest, the Waawaate-bot stepped neatly out of the way and disarmed the Behemoth. The AI flung the cannon so hard it flew far above the tree canopy and could be heard landing in the distance with a dull thud.

"What do you want?" the Behemoth screamed. "Tell Bugz I don't want to bother her anymore!" With this, he turned and ran down the trail, leaving his rucksack behind. As he pushed through the branches and leaves at a full sprint, he heard a noise beside him. He looked to his left and saw the Waawaate-bot sprinting on a parallel course, making eye contact the whole time. The effect of being hunted by this twisted-mouth demon scared him badly enough. However, the Behemoth couldn't help but think about the huge crypto balance tied to his account that hung in the balance. If he couldn't evade this tormentor, or even if he logged out, he'd lose it all.

"You can run, but you can't hide," the bot said. "It's a cliché, but it's true—at least in this case."

The Behemoth stopped on a dime and sprinted back up the trail in the direction he'd just come. When he looked behind, he could see the Waawaate-bot gaining ground. When he looked to his right, the bot was already there. He glanced to his left and the AI appeared there as well. The Behemoth couldn't figure out a way to change what was happening.

The Behemoth pushed through the edge of the dense forest and in an instant was bathed in daylight. He saw the Waawaate-bot standing at the cliff's edge in front of him. The Behemoth tried to stop and turn again, only to find the bot was blocking his retreat back into the forest. As the Clan:LESS soldier scanned his options from left to right he saw a seeming multiplicity of Waawaate-bots quickly appearing, disappearing, and reappearing all around him in countless different locations. The images of the bots closed in tighter and tighter and left the Behemoth with only one possible means of escape. He ran toward the cliff—such a move had worked for Bugz in one of their epic battles. But just as he approached the edge, the Waawaate-bot clotheslined him and he fell roughly to the ground.

Sky filled the Behemoth's view as he struggled to regain his bearings. He was so out of sorts that he hadn't yet realized what had hit him when he saw the fateful words appear across the screen.

"You've been eliminated by Waawaate-iban. You cannot respawn at this time."

As he processed the news, the face of the bot appeared on screen, flashing its crooked grin.

The Behemoth deactivated the Spirit World in his VR visor and returned to the augmented reality version of the Floraverse. He was back in the living room of his bachelor apartment. He could see his gaming rig and high-end webcam in front of him. *A lot of good that will do me now,* he thought as he realized he'd have nothing to stream. When he respawned, he'd have a generic 'Versona, with a boring skin, and none of the cool weapons he'd spent so much time acquiring.

"GOD!" He pounded the table in front of him, still wearing his VR headset.

The Behemoth stared at the table for a breath before pounding it again five times in quick succession. He registered the pain in his hands. Frustration coursed through his body—he wished he could rage-quit inside the 'Verse, but there wouldn't even be any subscribers watching him who could reward his performative shouting with some crypto. He counted up the millions of followers and tens of thousands of dollars he'd just lost. He slammed his other fist on the table in front of him for good measure.

"Take it easy, bud," a now-familiar voice said. "You're going to break your hand." The Behemoth struggled to think of how the voice could've followed him here. "You might even break that nice gaming desk."

The Behemoth spun in his high-end gaming chair, hoping to debunk the obvious truth of the situation. As he stared through his AR goggles, he could see his pursuer directly in front of him.

There, in the middle of the Behemoth's condo, in apparent defiance of all known laws governing players of the Floraverse, was the Waawaate-bot, smiling his crooked grin.

"Like I said. You can run . . ." The bot took a step forward as his words trailed off.

CHAPTER 20

Waawaate, the real Waawaate, walked along a starry path, his fresh moccasins kicking up stardust as he moved silently forward. He looked to his left and saw a blue light that had been trailing him for as long as he could remember. *Has it always been there, even when I walked on Earth?* he asked himself. He could not recall the answer.

The sound of water stopped him in his tracks. It was something more than the sound of a creek streaming in the spring with all the runoff of the melted snow, but something less than the roaring rapids that dotted some of the rivers that came near the Rez. He tried to picture the Rez, but came away with nothing. He looked off to his right and studied the infinite blackness of space, dotted here and there with stars that burned more brilliantly than he expected. He was about to look back the way he'd come, but quickly snapped his gaze forward when he recalled the ghastly sight he'd seen the last time he'd looked back along his celestial path.

Far ahead of him, through the fog of the Milky Way, he could see movement. It looked as though the stars were melting, though instead of falling below, they appeared to run along some unseen surface and travel from left to right in front of him. *This is where the sound of water is coming from.* As he squinted to get a closer look at this river in the night sky, he realized the current was broken in a space directly in front of him. Here, there was a writhing mass of blackness. He couldn't make anything out beyond that.

Waawaate reached into his pocket and retrieved some tobacco to offer to the path on which he walked. As he finished his prayer offering, he found his moccasins carrying him—suddenly, he was flying forward at a speed so fast the stars around him began to move.

Waawaate recognized what the black, writhing mass was. He recoiled. He tried desperately to plant his moccasins on the starry path in a furious attempt to slow himself down. He traveled with such speed, surely multiple times the speed of light, that for the first few moments, his moccasins merely slid along on the road beneath him. Eventually, they found some traction and he came skidding to a halt directly before a sight that froze him with fear.

As Waawaate stood entirely still, the head of a giant jet-black saber-toothed cat snapped at him with its immense fangs, like a rabid dog on the end of a chain. The beast gnashed and roared in complete silence. Waawaate's fear petrified him such that he couldn't step backward. He was helpless to move in any direction as the beast lunged forward, trying to devour him, coming only inches from his face. As it moved from side to side, struggling to find a way free from whatever was keeping it bound to the other side of the stream, Waawaate could see the beast's snake-like body. Waawaate had recognized it instantly, but he still couldn't quite believe it. It was the creature that legend had warned him about since he was too young to remember. The monster that his sister had tamed in her adventures in the Floraverse.

Mishi-pizhiw.

Waawaate named the beast in his mind, yet there was no recognition from the supernatural creature in front of him. It continued to leap forward and test the limits of its reach, relentless in its desire to feast on Waawaate.

After enough time passed to reveal that Mishi-pizhiw was not going to be able to reach him, at least for the moment, Waawaate looked to his left. The starry night flowed like a river, one that began so far in the distance that he could not see its origin. The sound of the babbling brook now seemed a distant memory. The river roared by with the volume and ferocity of whitewater, though its surface was the same midnight black as the backdrop of the universe, punctuated by the same glowing fires. He traced the river of stars from left to right.

As he looked to the right of Mishi-pizhiw, he saw count-less moccasins, tobacco pouches, and knives littering the shores of this night torrent.

Waawaate understood the significance. If he tried to make it through the river to get around Mishi-pizhiw, it would be the end of his journey. He also knew he could not go back. He would not dare to turn around, for he knew the supposed bride he'd left behind would be wait-ing. He felt the hairs on his neck stand on end.

He looked at the beast that roared in front of him, giant black fangs reflecting the lights of the universe around them as the creature raged. With nowhere to turn, Waawaate's plan began to take shape.

The only way around it is through it. He breathed deeply. *Just like most challenges.*

Waawaate nodded and reached for his tobacco once more. He shut his eyes and dug deep to utter the most purely intended prayer he could muster. He placed the tobacco into the river and beseeched the underwater serpent to let him cross. He opened his eyes, genuinely expecting the monster to be still, as though he'd just solved some sort of riddle.

Instead, the beast roared more furiously than before and struck forward at Waawaate five times in rapid suc-cession, like an enraged cobra. Waawaate huffed in resignation and crossed his arms. Perhaps this is where he would spend the rest of time, trapped between trials and the never-ending unfolding of the universe.

With the relaxed tone of one who has always been there, he heard the guttural voice of the Black-Anishinaabe Elder speak to him again. "Gego zegiziken." *Don't be scared*, he translated to himself.

At this, he shook his head. *Is that it?* He studied the raging beast. *Is that all?* Waawaate shook his head again and sucked his teeth.

Waawaate leapt. As he jumped, he felt his moccasins carry him high above the raging beast's head. Mishipizhiw tried to bend over backward to trap Waawaate in his jaws, but he couldn't manage the contortion. Instead, the young Anishinaabe landed on its back like a ninja in a defensive crouch.

Waawaate looked to his left and then to his right and saw the river continuing to roar on by. But now, the beast had stopped writhing.

Waawaate stood and saw that the body of the snake had been transformed into a smooth black tree, like the inner core of ebony, though much larger than a tree trunk that would exist on Earth. Waawaate looked behind him and saw the corpse bride watching him from the far shore, trapped in her place. He ran the length of the tree and hopped down onto the side opposite from the road he'd been on, which resumed its course on this new side of the river.

Waawaate looked back a final time. At the far end of the black tree was no monster's head. Instead, the gargantuan ebony terminated in a mess of roots that sprawled up and down and every which way along the far banks of the river. It looked like the big trees did in the forests back home after they'd been uprooted and knocked down by a storm.

As he turned to resume walking down the starry path, Waawaate couldn't be certain whether he'd ever seen Mishi-pizhiw or whether he'd merely been face-to-face with a black tree the whole time. He shook his head and looked to the path ahead of him.

CHAPTER 21

After a call home from the vice-principal's office and a scolding for disrupting class time, Bugz's parents took her phone away from her for a full twenty-four hours. For the entirety of this period, isolated from her device, she felt as though she had an itch she needed to scratch but couldn't reach, and it bothered her tremendously.

As soon as she got her phone back, Bugz ran to her room and returned to the Floraverse. Yet less than a breath after she'd logged back in, before she'd even landed on the shores of Lake of the Torches, much less had a chance to scratch the itch that had tormented her, the Waawaate-bot transported himself directly in front of her. She was too surprised to hide the annoyed look on her face as the bot began to speak.

"Bugz!" the AI began. "I've been waiting forever for you to get back here. Guess what?" The bot barely gave

Bugz a chance to open her mouth before he spoke again. "I know where Alpha is in the Spirit World. Let's go get him right now!"

"How do you know that?" Bugz had a sixth sense for the way things unfolded in the 'Verse, one she'd honed over her years playing the game, but it wasn't anywhere near a surveillance system that let her know all the other players' whereabouts. Bugz wondered how the bot had learned this new skill.

"Never mind that. Let's go get him!"

"Actually, I was really hoping to build up our forces with some more supernatural creatures. Remember that Thunderbird I was trying to show you?"

The Waawaate-bot interrupted her again and pressured her to go on the offensive against her long-time enemy. Bugz tried to manage her frustration by reminding herself why she'd created this AI in the first place. Working on it had been her outlet throughout her brother's sickness. Whenever she felt worn down or sad from visiting Waawaate in the hospital, she'd dive into the 'Verse and work on this simulation of him. It had started as a simple thing to distract her, a way to play with her phone to escape her feelings. But over the months of his illness, it had come to mean so much more to her, this replica who looked like Waawaate as she remembered him, not like the frail person he'd become.

Bugz studied the bot's face—he really did look like Waawaate, even if he now appeared frazzled, with stray strands of hair sticking out in a way her brother never would've tolerated. The bot sported a desperate smile that belied the calm and natural style of the real Waawaate. Bugz concluded that, as she'd forged the bot, she must've cranked up the attributes she found most memorable in her brother too high. Her brother's energy, enthusiasm, and effortless charm now came off in this facsimile as irritating, relentless, and trying too hard. Still, Bugz didn't want to pull the plug on this project . . . at least not yet. She felt the bot could be saved.

Bugz walked along the pebble beach and toward the gathering spot where she knew she could find virtual birds. She noted the day's soft, gray, cloud-covered hue. It seemed to match her mood as the bot pestered her throughout her stroll, teleporting to her right and left, in front of her and then behind her with the manic energy of a toddler.

"Okay, fine!" Bugz raised her voice with the realization she wouldn't get any of her plans done today.

"Let's go then?" The bot looked to her expectantly.

"Skoden," she relented.

At this, the bot grabbed her hand. Instantly, Bugz felt as though she'd been knocked flat on her back and had her stomach pulled forward at the speed of light. Her surroundings warped into a blur. Before she could recognize what was happening, the strong motion stopped suddenly. Bugz found herself holding hands with the bot in the tree line overlooking a mountain vista. Somehow, he'd dragged her along through that teleportation thing he'd figured out how to do, instantly transporting her to a distant part of the Floraverse.

"There he is," the Waawaate-bot whispered.

Bugz squinted as she studied the figure swinging a pickax in front of them. It was clearly Alpha. The eight-foot height, the exaggerated musculature. She could even see his different-colored eyes from this distance. But he was alone, with no clanmates around, and only one lonely laser blaster nearby laying just out of arm's reach. Bugz felt the tiniest bit of sympathy for him as he worked, oblivious to them. Even if he had destroyed the real Thunderbird's Nest close to her home in the real world, she still recognized how vulnerable he was at the moment. She shook her head.

"Ready?" the bot asked.

"I don't think it's worth it. Look at him. Where's the sport in—"

Before Bugz could complete her thought, the bot had transported himself directly behind Alpha. As her sworn enemy raised his pickax in a backswing, expecting to bring it down on the pile of valuable ore in front of him, the Waawaate-bot snatched the tool and flung it into the sky, where it disappeared beyond the horizon.

Alpha took off sprinting immediately. This was a doomed plan, as the bot merely teleported to a spot in his path. Bugz shouted at the bot to come get her. Reacting to her voice, the bot looked away from Alpha for a moment, which allowed the Clan:LESS leader to push him out of the way and gain a step in the process.

The bot shrugged, shifted himself to a location just next to Bugz, and dragged her through the virtual space-time of the 'Verse to another spot just ahead of Alpha.

"Wow, that feels so weird," Bugz said, sounding legitimately ill.

With Bugz's attention momentarily diverted, the Waawaate-bot snatched Alpha around the waist and, in one fluid motion, suplexed him to the ground. The force of the impact sent a shockwave rolling through the ground—and Alpha's gamertag floating slowly toward the sky. He'd been eliminated.

The Waawaate-bot raised his fist, preparing to strike the lifeless 'Versona lying on the ground. Bugz ran forward and tackled him. Bugz and the bot rolled twice before coming to a rest in a heap. As she stood, Bugz could see the look of shock on the bot's face.

"He's finished," she said. "We don't need to take it too far, okay?"

The bot stood and dusted himself off before finding Bugz's eyes again. "I'm going to follow him home."

Bugz lunged for the bot. Bugz still hated Clan:LESS for everything they'd done to her in the past, but she also felt she had to stop the bot. As she dove forward, Bugz felt time slowing down. In this warped moment, Bugz saw the bot's arms and legs grow to be as long as tree trunks, his head fading from her vision. In this slow motion, she succeeded in grabbing his ankle.

Instantly, Bugz felt as though she were being dragged through a lake's worth of water as she held on for dear life, even as her sense of direction completely deserted her.

For a time, she couldn't make sense of what she was seeing. The three dimensions of the Spirit World appeared to split apart and reveal an additional plane of existence. She couldn't discern it clearly for all the light flooding her eyes. Before she blinked, she thought she made out an image that evoked graph paper and spiderwebs, a tangled mess of interconnected points.

Like the recoil of an elastic band snapping, she had the feeling of being propelled back in the other direction. Her stomach still felt as though it were spinning inside her.

Bugz looked around and realized with some disappointment that she was still at the base of that mountain next to the vanquished Alpha. The Waawaate-bot had slipped her grasp.

Bugz jumped in the air and began the long flight back to Lake of the Torches.

CHAPTER 22

Feng watched Bugz pace back and forth in his bedroom in the real world. He sat on his bed, back against the wall with his legs out in front of him. He jiggled them distractedly as he listened to Bugz vent about everything that was going wrong in the 'Verse. His competing feelings about the Waawaate-bot swung back and forth inside of him. He wanted to confess that he'd felt uneasy and had only held back because he didn't want to hurt her. A moment later, he felt like explaining to her how much the AI had helped him build his monument to the children. *I'd still be picking away at that rock and dangling from a cliff if it wasn't for him,* Feng thought. A knock at the door interrupted the pendulum in his heart.

"Come in," he said curtly.

Liumei popped her head in as though checking to see if the coast was clear. "Hope I'm not disturbing anything."

"No, we're just talking," Bugz said, as she sat at the foot of the bed. Liumei nodded and entered before Bugz added, "Actually, I'm doing all the talking. Feng's just sitting there looking bored."

"Active listening, Feng. You'd be surprised how far it goes," his aunt said, shooting Bugz a knowing smile. She sat on the bed, bringing a silence into the room.

"So, what's up?" Feng asked, crossing his legs underneath himself to sit up straighter.

"Well, I wanted to show you something." Liumei withdrew her phone from her pocket. "It's kind of . . . sensitive." Feng felt a nervous rush wash over him. He didn't want to ask what she meant.

"Should I . . ." Bugz looked at the door, but Liumei shook her head and shifted to face Feng more fully.

"It's about your parents, Feng."

Feng felt the need to stand. At the same time, he didn't want either Bugz or his aunt to see how affected he was by the last video he'd seen of his parents, the one in which they'd said some awful things. That had shaken something loose inside of him. He turned his back to the other two and began to carefully examine the eagle-bone whistle necklace that hung from a nail on his wall.

This beautiful instrument, carved from the wing bone of a golden eagle, had been given to Feng by Bugz's mother in a Sweat Lodge the year prior. Feng felt transported back to the darkness of that lodge, the intense heat, the emotions that roiled inside his heart. The loneliness he felt believing his parents had chosen to leave him behind. The emptiness in his spirit at believing the lies the party had told him. The confusion at seeing the pride of the Indigenous Peoples of North America after being taught all his life that Indigenous Peoples should be ashamed of who they were.

Liumei cleared her throat and put her phone away. "All I wanted to say, Feng, is that we have to remember that video you saw was propaganda, and doesn't reflect what your parents really think or feel." His aunt cleared her throat again.

Feng reached out and ran his finger along the beadwork that was wrapped around the middle of the whistle. The beads were small, a sign of a good craftsperson. He focused on the feeling of the small ridges formed by the rows of beads passing under his finger as he heard his aunt speak again.

"Anyway, your uncle, my brother, noticed a newspaper visible on the table behind them. It's a small local publication, put out by the neighborhood committee of the party, of course." Feng turned in time to see Liumei pause and glance at Bugz, who appeared transfixed by the words. Feng knew what his aunt would say next and he beat her to it.

"He knows where they are?"

Liumei nodded. "Well, not one hundred percent, but he's pretty sure about which city they're in."

"Why can't he just search them up online? Message them?" Bugz asked, confusion visible in her arched brow.

"Uyghurs aren't allowed to use phones after they get out of the camps," Feng said, staring at the farthest corner in the room. He turned back to the eagle whistle. He heard his aunt stand and felt her hand on his shoulder.

"Feng," she began in a tender voice. "Uncle's on his way to go find them."

Feng felt a hope he'd long hidden welling up inside. He surprised himself with the tremble in his voice when he spoke. "I'll ask the Waawaatę-bot to find them. He can travel through the online world more quickly than Uncle can travel in the real world. Even if Mom and Dad don't have a phone, he can find them on surveillance cameras or something."

"No," Bugz said. The word felt like an insult as Feng heard it. He turned to see her looking to the floor, a serious expression on her face.

Feng wondered whether she understood what she was saying. "You don't want me to find my parents?"

"Of course I do," Bugz replied. "But haven't you been listening? The bot is out of control. We have to stop him. Asking him to do something for us, a favor, is the last thing we should be doing right now."

"My parents are alive!" Feng stopped as he realized he was much closer to shouting than he'd intended. He sighed and tried to sound more reasonable. "All I'm saying is, I don't think the bot's so bad. At least . . . maybe this would give him a chance to show us he can do something good."

Bugz shot Feng a look, as though she were now the injured party. Liumei stepped between the two of them. "Well, we don't have to decide anything right now. I'll tell Uncle we're on board with his plan, and you two can sort out whatever it is that needs sorting out."

CHAPTER 23

"Honestly, it's not even fun anymore," Bugz huffed to Stormy as they met up in the emptying hallway of their school. Homeroom had just finished and the kids from town were heading home, leaving the Rez kids to wander the disinfectant-smelling halls until the buses came to drive them home six hours later. This difference in schooling was a by-product of the old school restrictions from the pandemics that let kids who lived nearby attend remotely if they so chose, and forced those who had to bus to school to attend in person. "The 'Verse has always been my escape. The place where I get to be me, my getaway. Where I go to have fun." Stormy nodded as Bugz continued. Up until this conversation, Bugz had only shared the existence of the bot with Feng. But with things going so haywire, she felt she had to tell Stormy. "Now it feels like a chore. Like I just have to entertain the AI brother I made." She chuckled without any apparent joy. "God, that's weird—AI brother. He's actually nothing like my brother . . . even though I tried to make them exactly the same."

"Nobody could be like Waawaate." Stormy looked away from Bugz. They turned a corner into the library and found a table. As she slid her book bag onto the table, she retrieved a bottle of lemonade from inside and took a sip. Bugz gestured with her chin. Stormy smiled back and cleared her throat. "What?" Stormy had the look of a kid who'd just been caught sneaking popsicles from the freezer.

"You, that's what." Bugz shook her head with a chuckle. "Still jonesin' for lemonade?"

"What? It's good." Stormy offered her the bottle, but Bugz waved it off.

Bugz sighed. "I feel like quitting the Floraverse."

Stormy looked up from her bottle with hope in her eyes. "Really? That's not so bad. I mean, it could give you a chance to do more stuff in the real world."

"Like what?"

"Like there's a party tonight. Wanna come?"

Bugz felt her nerves boil beneath the surface of the calm exterior she focused on projecting. She asked as many questions as she could think of, anything to try to delay giving her friend a definite answer.

"Bugz, it'll be fun. It's on the Rez. You'll know everyone there. Bring Feng. I'm sure he'll like it."

"Okay," Bugz said, a lightness overtaking her. "Can we all go together? Like, show up at the same time?"

Stormy chuckled and told Bugz it'd be no problem.

"I'm sorry." Bugz felt her face getting hot and tried to smile through it. "It's not really my scene. Just come with me and tell me it'll be alright."

"Sure, and I'll even do all the talking for you once we get there."

"Deal."

CHAPTER 24

The low end of the music rumbled in the ground beneath their feet as Bugz followed Feng and Stormy up the gravel approach to the house where the party was already in full swing. In the twilight, Bugz could make out a few people on the wooden stairs, sharing a vape. Bugz took a deep breath and paused a few steps behind her friend.

"You coming?" Stormy asked with a smile.

Bugz blew the air from her lungs out through pursed lips and hurried to catch up. As she sneaked by the group on the stairs, she was relieved that they simply nodded and smiled at her. Feng held the screen door open, but Bugz still rushed through it as though it might slam shut on her.

Once inside, the music boomed louder and more clearly. A steady rabble of loud conversation floated over top of the beat, thanks to the partygoers, and the occasional loud clink of glass could be heard. Bugz scanned the room. After she'd given it the once over, she saw Stormy hugging their host. He was a tall basketball player who'd been in her brother's class. When Stormy let go of their embrace, he smiled to Feng and Bugz. Bugz nodded nervously, feeling almost territorial as she wondered about the nature of the relationship between him and Stormy. But Stormy was already talking to someone else, and she wasn't glancing back at the ball player. Maybe they were just friends.

"Hey, thanks for coming," the baller said.

"No problem, we're glad to be here," Bugz said nervously.

"Huh?" he asked back in a loud voice still drowned out by the dance music thumping from large speakers across the living room.

"Thanks for having us!" Bugz shouted, just as the music stopped. Her gaze fell to her feet immediately, an embarrassed smile shooting across her face. She could hear giggles from across the space as the good-natured teasing common in Anishinaabe communities kicked in.

"We're glad you could make it too, Bugz!" one young woman said through a wide smile.

"Wow, you know you take parties for granted until someone new shows up and appreciates it so much! How refreshing!" the young woman's boyfriend offered. He raised his red Solo cup. "Cheers, Bugz!"

"Shut up!" Bugz shot back, laughing at herself. The room descended into head nods and stuck-out tongues, a universal Indigenous sign for a joke well-received. She shook her head at herself as the beat to the next song kicked in.

"That wasn't *too* awkward," Feng said with a slight grin as the music swallowed the sounds in the room again.

Their host stepped in closer to them. "What are you drinking?" he asked.

"Just G Fuel," Bugz answered, holding up her energy drink. The host looked to Feng, who did the same, and finally to Stormy.

"I'm good," she replied.

"Going straight edge tonight, right on!" the host said.

Bugz nodded her head to the music before deciding to spark up conversation. "Where are your parents?"

"They're quarantining in the city. They just got back from a vacation overseas, so they'll be there for a while," he said as the smile returned to his face. "So I figured, might as well have a party now. At least I'll have a week to clean up." The baller looked across the room, shook his head, and leaned closer to Bugz. "Don't let what those people are saying about you online bother you. You didn't do anything wrong. All of us deserve a chance to dance."

Bugz smiled in response and took a sip of her energy drink. Over the course of the next five or six songs, the crowd inside the house grew noticeably. By the time the sky outside the large bay windows turned completely black, the kitchen, living room, and dining room had become a hot, humid, standing-room-only dance floor. Bugz, Feng, and Stormy continued to hold up the wall, nodding their heads for the most part to the beat and waving to people they knew. And even as lots of friends stopped to talk to Stormy, she remained true to her word, and didn't abandon Bugz. Finally, the playlist cued up an old-school dance track mixed with pow-wow singing that everyone at the party recognized, except for Feng. A chorus of screams, yells, and war cries went up over the crowd.

Bugz wasn't sure if it was the caffeine in her energy drink kicking in or just the excitement of the party, but she suddenly tossed her head back and let out a long, loud ululation. Almost surprised with herself, she looked to Stormy, who stopped for a beat before lelele-ing right back at her. A few other young women nearby joined in, and the sound of the war cry of women from Indigenous nations around the world pierced the dance music. This provoked another round of shouting and yelling from the rest of the rowdy crowd.

"There you go, missy," Stormy said with a huge smile. "Might as well," she continued, gesturing to the dance floor with a nod of her head.

"Alright." Bugz grinned, following Stormy through the packed crowd and dragging Feng by the hand behind her. The trio found a spot close to the center of the impromptu arena. There wasn't much room to do anything other than jump along to the music and do their best to avoid the flailing arms and red cups that were being raised all around them. When the song ended, the crowd shouted for more.

Feng leaned into Bugz and asked, "What was that?"

"'Electric Pow Wow.' It's old-school."

He nodded in reply and stood up straight again when the crowd started jumping to the next beat. Bugz raised her hands above her head, closed her eyes, and lost herself in the music.

Song after song, melody after melody, chorus after chorus, Bugz jumped in time with the music, adding a dance move with her feet or arms here and there when there was space in the crowd to do so.

From time to time, she'd make eye contact with Feng and they'd dance together. As they did, her heart raced with feelings for him. While she cared about him deeply, she was still upset he hadn't taken her seriously about the dangers of the Waawaate-bot. She trusted him. Why didn't he trust *her*? But now that they were having fun together, dancing, yelling, jumping with a bunch of people from school, those negative thoughts faded and positive ones took their place. Feng looked like he was having fun too. Maybe not as much as her—he still seemed like he was holding back a bit—but he made no move to leave the dance floor.

Bugz felt the way she did at a pow-wow—the visceral feeling of dancing, the emotional lift of the music, and the social rush of being around others.

As the beat dropped on one of Bugz's favorite songs, she looked to Feng. She studied his facial features. His skin was a shade lighter than Stormy's. She peered into his eyes, noting their shape, much like her own. When he looked back at her, she made no move to turn away. Instead, Bugz bit her lower lip, smiled, and pulled him closer. The beat changed, a new song started, and the two went back to jumping in time with the music with all their friends.

When Stormy leaned in and told her she was tired and needed to take a break, Bugz simply nodded and handed over her hoodie, asking if she could hang on to it for her. What went unsaid, but was clear to both, was how happy Bugz was that Stormy had dragged her to the party in the first place.

Other kids her age from the Rez that she usually only saw at school now smiled at her and raised their drinks. Bugz smiled and they nodded back. She felt she'd been inducted into a secret society. Had these people been having fun like this without her all along? She wondered what it was that had held her back from doing this sort of thing before. *Why'd I always run to the 'Verse?* she asked herself. *This is so much fun.*

Feng took a break shortly after Stormy and joined her in leaning against the same wall they'd stood against earlier. This freed Bugz to join another group of young women she'd grown up with but hadn't spoken to much since they'd started high school. Not that they spoke much now either. They simply danced and sang along to the anthems that played back-to-back on the party play-list. Bugz felt herself becoming a sweaty mess, but she didn't mind—everyone else in the party looked the same. There were infinite shades of Anishinaabe skin tones all glistening in the low red light that covered the main area of the house party.

Finally, after what could've been days but was proba-bly more like an hour or two, Bugz relented and found her way back to Feng and Stormy.

"Wow." Stormy flashed a grin. "Who knew? You were secretly a party animal all along. We just needed to let you out of your cage."

"It's always the quiet ones," Feng chuckled.

Bugz shook her head and asked for her hoodie back. She wiped her face with it and tied it around her waist. When Stormy told them she wasn't feeling one hundred percent, the group decided to leave. They passed the host and his inner circle of friends. After several rounds of elbow bumps, head nods, and promises to do it all again soon, they finally made their way to the pile of shoes at the front door.

Bugz pushed the screen door open and felt the rush of cool early-summer air run over her sweat-covered skin. She ran down the wooden steps, closed her eyes, and reached for the sky, stretching her arms as far as they could go. She felt invigorated and happy, and said a quiet prayer of thanks for the new experience.

When she opened her eyes, Bugz could see the Milky Way spilled out across the night sky. As her eyes adjusted to the low light, she absorbed it even more clearly—not just the millions of stars shining brilliantly, but also the nebulous fog that seemed to be set in the background at a distance much further than any of the twinkling lights.

Bugz smiled and waited for her friends to catch up to her.

"I miss Waawaate," she said.

"We all do," Stormy answered, taking Bugz's hand into her own. She sniffed quickly and brushed her cheek.

Bugz looked to Feng and found him staring at his phone with a puzzled look on his face. "What is it?" she asked.

"I'm getting a video call from a strange number."

"Unknown?"

"No, it says who it is," Feng answered. "I just didn't expect to hear from them . . ."

CHAPTER 25

"Hello?" Feng sounded uncertain. He paused on the gravel road outside the house party, the rocks beneath his feet crunching as he shifted his weight back and forth, impatient for the video call to connect. He glanced quickly at Bugz and Stormy, who held hands on the road in front of him. They eyed him quizzically.

"Who the heck calls at this hour?" Feng heard Bugz ask.

"Better not be his other girlfriend," Stormy joked.

"Stop!" Bugz said, sounding embarrassed.

Feng looked back to his phone and saw a tired, frazzled face that was very familiar to him. It was the Behemoth—his former clanmate and one of his closest friends, or at least he *had* been a close friend until Feng left Clan:LESS and chose to ride with Bugz instead.

"Feng? Are you there?" the Behemoth asked.

Feng angled the phone so his face could be seen in the distant illumination of the porch light from the house they'd just left. "Yeah, it's me, man."

"Oh good, hey . . ." The Behemoth paused, clearly unsure of how to broach the subject he wanted to address.

"What can I do for you?" Feng wondered why he'd adopted a formal tone to try and cover up what he was now feeling. Clan:LESS had harassed him and trolled him for months after he'd left their ranks.

"Listen, this is going to sound super desperate, but don't hang up. I need your help. It won't take long." The Behemoth quickly glanced from side to side. "I can't stay on the call much longer anyways."

Feng paused.

The Behemoth continued in a rapid, syncopated cadence that only added to Feng's impression that his old friend was not well. "I need your help, because I think I'm losing it. I haven't slept in two days . . . and before that, I didn't rest much either. I can't go to the 'Verse, I can't stay home, I can't leave the house. I can't look at my phone. No matter where I go, there's no escape."

"Slow down, man," Feng said seriously. "What's going on?"

"There's no time to explain."

"Well, why are you asking me for help?" Feng scowled as he said this. "Honestly, we both know we're not close anymore."

"You're the only one who can help—"

Feng interrupted. "And why would I help? After what you guys did to me? It was relentless. You can't look at *your* phone? That's what it was like for me."

"C'mon, Feng, I wouldn't do this unless I absolutely had to." The Behemoth looked to be on the verge of tears. "You're the only one who can help, well . . . one of the only ones who can help. Besides, you know that wasn't me. I didn't send memes. I didn't troll."

Feng looked up from his phone, weighing the veracity of this statement against the heavier truth that even if the Behemoth hadn't actively harassed Feng online, he hadn't spoken out against it or defended Feng in any way.

Bugz raised her chin to Feng as though asking what was going on.

Feng looked back to his phone and asked the Behemoth to cut to the chase.

"He's everywhere . . . everywhere I look. He won't let me sleep. He won't let me think. He's always there. Even when I turn my phone off, he finds a way to appear on a screen nearby—my computer, a monitor in a window I'm walking by. Besides, you know I can't turn my phone off. That makes me even more stressed."

Feng scrunched his forehead. "What do you mean 'he'? Who are you talking about?"

"Him!" the Behemoth shouted through the phone. "Her brother! The one with the Indigenous clothing and the crooked mouth. He hasn't left me alone for weeks. He's always there in my room in the darkness, waiting for me the second I turn a device on." The Behemoth looked to his feet and shook his head in self-pity.

Feng looked to Bugz, who now let go of Stormy's hand and walked toward Feng with a concerned look on her face. As she arrived at his side, Feng heard screaming from his phone.

"He's here! He's here! He's back! I've got to turn the phone off."

The video call terminated abruptly and left Feng staring at the transparent piece of glass in his hand.

CHAPTER 26

From the moment Bugz put her headset on and logged back in to the 'Verse, she was shocked. She double-checked her location on the map in her heads-up display several times to confirm she had in fact relaunched her 'Versona in Lake of the Torches, her virtual home base, a place she assumed had summer weather every day. Sure enough, that was her location, no matter how different it looked from what she'd always known.

Bugz scanned the windswept surface of the frozen Lake of the Torches. A cold, hard wind blew snow across the virtual glacier. Large sheets of ice lay on top of each other where the swirling water beneath had caused the surface to heave and buckle. It gave the lake the messy look of a giant children's playground. Bugz licked her lips as she processed all that had changed in the 'Verse since her last time online just the day before, prior to the party.

Overnight, a virtual ice age had descended on one of her favorite places anywhere.

She stood in a black, fur-lined parka. Feng stepped forward so he could speak softly to her. "I thought this was the land of eternal summer," he whispered.

"It is." Bugz could hear the wind howling in the distance. "It was. I told you the bot was a problem." She looked over her shoulder at the sound of snow crunching behind them. "It's him."

As Feng turned to follow the sound, a white hare emerged from behind a block of ice and studied them carefully through red eyes. It tapped its feet twice and sprang away, lost in the white winter wasteland. "It's just a rabbit."

"Don't be fooled." Bugz began trudging through deep snow toward the center of the lake. "He's watching us. He just doesn't want to show himself." She raised her voice as though trying to taunt the Waawaate-bot. The snow became harder to traverse and Bugz sank to her hips in a deep drift. She turned to Feng, who gave her an exasperated look as he found himself similarly trapped in another patch of snow. "Here." Bugz raised her arm and two branches flew into her outstretched hand from an ash tree near the shore.

After she threw them at Feng, the branches curled into snowshoes in midair before landing in front of him. He struggled to put them on for a moment before Bugz sighed and gathered two more branches. In a fluid motion, she rolled to her back, affixed the branches-turned-snowshoes to the soles of her boots, and rocked back forward to her feet. Standing on top of the snow, she looked down at Feng with a smirk. "Want me to tie yours up for you too?"

Bugz began closing the distance to the center of the lake rapidly. After much grunting, struggling, and thrashing around in the snow, Feng followed her. The wind seemed to grow bitterly cold and howled as it picked up in intensity. Bugz shuddered, though she knew this experience was entirely simulated. No matter what she told herself, her mind had trouble separating the virtual from reality.

The pair made a good pace as they traversed the surface of the icy Lake of the Torches. In the center, they could see a massive ice formation that resembled a crystal palace. As they approached the halfway point, the ice began to creak wearily. They exchanged a worried look and froze. The ice waited only a breath before screaming in reply. Several sheets of frozen water broke apart beneath their feet and began spiraling around them. Before Bugz and Feng could react, a whirlpool of jagged glacier- and ice-water spun furiously around them.

Kicking her feet free from the snowshoes, Bugz began sprinting and jumping from ice floe to ice floe as they cycloned around her. Her movement had the effect of a runner on a treadmill turned to full-speed as she barely kept up with the spinning water thrashing in every direction. Finally, she pulled ahead in the race and ran up the side of the frozen whirlpool to freedom.

From the edge of the ice, Bugz turned to shout back to Feng. As she did, she was silenced by the sight that greeted her.

At the base of the cyclone was a giant humanoid figure composed entirely of ice. The ice giant screamed as Feng tried to crawl and scratch his way up the spiraling vortex of frost with futility. The monster reached up and pulled Feng down to the base of the frozen lake. Bugz watched helplessly through the ice as the giant took off running beneath the water in the direction of the crystal castle.

Immediately, the ice shelf on which Bugz stood began to collapse further. She had no choice but to run toward the place Feng was being taken.

At a full sprint, Bugz glanced back. For every step she took, the ice collapsed just as quickly behind her, the smooth white surface breaking up into massive blocks before disappearing below. Bugz grimaced and pushed her pace even faster.

CHAPTER 27

A light above sparked a small fire on the ceiling and Feng could see again. Since he'd been dragged off by the giant, he'd been unable to move from his location or study his surroundings. He knew he hadn't been eliminated from the Floraverse . . . just taken to a place where he was, until a moment earlier, being held in total darkness.

As his eyes adjusted to the bizarre ceiling fire, Feng scanned the room. He struggled to make sense of what he saw. His old clanmates were trapped in ice all around him. Alpha was preserved in a state of shock with his arms out, trying to reach for help. Gym and Joe were both frozen with their arms at their sides, as though they'd been caught completely unaware. Feng ticked off the names of the other Clan:LESS soldiers embedded in the walls of ice until he finally made his way to the warrior closest to him, on his left. There, trapped with a look of horror on his face and with his arms raised to block whatever terrible sight he'd beheld, was the Behemoth.

Feng pondered this and looked to his feet—they were buried in ice that stapled him to the floor.

Suddenly, a hooded figure entered the room, walking on the ceiling. At this, Feng realized he'd lost all sense of direction . . . he was actually hanging upside down. Just as quickly, his head began to spin and he felt a sickness send the room spiraling all around him. This vertigo had apparently only been held off by his confusion. Now that his brain had regained a sense of up and down, it was sending all of his internal systems into a scrambled state as they tried to make sense of what was going on. The fact that this was occurring inside a VR headset made it that much more disorienting.

Amid this cacophony, the hooded figure stepped toward Feng.

Feng reached to rip his headset off for fear of vomiting. But the last thing he saw in the 'Verse before he did was unmistakable. Lit only by firelight, the figure lowered his hood and revealed to Feng his wicked, twisted grin.

Feng found himself back in his room in his aunt's house in the real world, clutching his phone and headset in his hands. He lay down immediately to try and stop the spinning sensation. He tried to close his eyes and focus only on the feel of the bed beneath him. Feng knew he'd be unable to go back into the 'Verse anytime soon. He'd had vertigo before in the real world and knew

that even if he did log back into the 'Verse he'd be use-
less, unable to navigate the virtual world or even tell up
from down.

Bugz would be on her own.

CHAPTER 28

From high atop the crystal palace, Bugz could see the ice giant running toward her from far away. She knew from texts that Feng had sent that he'd been captured by the AI and wouldn't be able to help.

The giant beast ran at a full stride, his legs lifting high off the frozen surface of Lake of the Torches, his arms pumping furiously. Bugz could feel the humongous ice crystals rumbling beneath her. With each step the giant took, the frost beneath her shook more violently. He left massive craters in the ice in his wake.

As the ice giant closed the distance with his final few steps, Bugz leapt off the high tower. She extended her left leg in midair and landed a hard Sparta kick directly to the beast's chest, which sent him stumbling backward. He landed with a violent crash that broke straight through the surface of the ice.

For all the shock visible on the ice giant's face at being bested by his relatively tiny foe, Bugz felt no mercy. As the beast sank slowly toward the lake floor, Bugz dove in and swam after him. She kicked furiously through the stream of air bubbles that raced back toward the surface. In the dim blue light, Bugz caught up to her prey and crouched on his chest just as he landed on the lake bed with a dull thud. Bugz pulled out her infinity war club and drew it back, preparing to strike the beast, just as the sediment kicked up by the impact clouded the waters around her. No gamertag rose from the shrouded lake water after Bugz eliminated the ice giant from the Floraverse. He'd been a creation of the Waawaate-bot.

She turned and swam toward the domed structure on the lake bed directly below the crystal palace.

CHAPTER 29

Bugz pushed through the doors to find herself staring over the top of a small fire directly into the wild eyes of the Waawaate-bot. His gaze stopped her in her tracks for a second before she refocused and stepped fully inside the room. She did her best to keep looking at the AI as she recognized the frozen figures of so many of her sworn enemies hanging like icicles from the ceiling of this wintry lodge.

"You must know that you're not doing good anymore," Bugz said, in her best attempt to put forward a calm, serious voice. It took all her focus not to betray the fear she felt throughout her body. She breathed in slowly and felt a tremor, which she tried to disguise with a stretch of her neck. "You turned the warmth into cold. Summer into winter." Her heart sank as the Waawaate-bot stepped to his left and revealed the latest victim he'd trapped in the ice.

"I know," the bot began. "But I am who I am." He turned and examined Feng's frozen features.

"This is wrong." Bugz spoke firmly and sternly. "This isn't what I created you for."

"Why did you create me?" The bot turned to face her again. "Wasn't I supposed to help you bring your brother back from the other side? Didn't you invite me to cross from the land of the dead back into the world of the living? You spoke to me as you made me."

"I didn't say that." Bugz felt a flash of guilt. All her life, she'd been taught to keep the living and the dead separated. A reminder was right there in her brother's name: Waawaate—the northern lights, the aurora representing those who've passed on, who must not be called back down to earth by whistling. The Elders had always told them not to whistle at night.

"'Come back to me,' you said." The bot leaned forward, sensing weakness. "Come back from where, huh? Come back to whom? You knew what you were doing, reaching across the divide."

The bot took a step closer to Bugz. She snapped out of her shame and responded in kind, eager not to show any fear to her creation.

"I invested everything I knew into you. I gave you my all. But I did it because I wanted you to be like him— my brother. The real Waawaate."

At this, the bot's crooked smile twisted into a foul grimace. His contorted face flashed with rage even as the left side of his mouth remained an unanswered question mark. "I *am* the real Waawaate!" the bot shouted.

"You're nothing like him." Bugz took another step forward and retrieved the infinity war club from her back. The ball at the end glinted in firelight even as the body of the club coursed with energy.

"I'm better than him." The bot teleported immediately behind Bugz to whisper in her ear. "I know why you really made me. Look at all that I've done."

Bugz spun quickly and swung the club, missing the bot, who teleported to the opposite side of the fire.

"Why do you want to hurt me? I thought you loved me. I thought you loved Waawaate."

"You're not Waawaate!"

The bot teleported to Bugz's side, took the infinity war club from her hands, and flung it into the fire before instantly moving back to his original position. "Won't you at least talk to me?"

"There's nothing to talk about. He told us what you were doing." Bugz pointed to the Behemoth's anguished face. "Look around. You're out of control." Images flashed in her mind as she imagined all the other Clan:LESS soldiers being tormented in the real world by visions of the Waawaate-bot on devices all around them.

"Clan:LESS? You hate them. Be honest. This is what you really created me to do," the bot said in a wounded-sounding voice. "What happened? Why are you losing your nerve?" The bot now adopted a genuinely curious tone.

"It shouldn't be like this." Bugz bit her lower lip. "They may have done terrible things to me in the 'Verse . . . even in the real world." She shook her head to emphasize the point. "But I always said I would hold myself to a higher standard." Bugz lowered her brow, even as her eyes remained locked on the bot. "But now, thanks to you, I'm no better than any of them."

The bot flashed forward and lifted Bugz high off the ground by her parka. With both hands, she grabbed his forearm and struggled to break free, lifting her legs off the ground as she tried to push off the bot's chest. As she did this, his crooked mouth returned to its creepy smile. "I see," the bot began. "You don't have what it takes to finish the job against Clan:LESS." He lifted Bugz higher. She struggled even more furiously at this, shaking his arm and trying to pry his fingers open, to no avail. "You hide behind noble talk, sure. But at the end of the day . . ."

"That's not true." Bugz grunted as she squirmed frantically to free herself.

"Yes, it is," the grinning bot said, raising Bugz directly above his head. "Now I see why you made me. To do your dirty work." He cocked his head slightly as he looked into her eyes. Bugz felt a shiver run down her spine. *How can an AI look into my soul like this?* she asked herself. "You made me so you could beat Clan:LESS once and for all—not just in the virtual world but everywhere, in the real world, in their minds, and in their hearts. Those are the real battlefields. You made me to ensure they'd never play again."

"No!"

"And you created me to do it so you could keep telling yourself you're living up to a higher standard . . . that it was someone else, another being, not you who'd done it. Through me you could torment your enemies without mercy, but then still lie to yourself and make believe you have a clean conscience." He cocked his head in the other direction. "So here I am, doing your dirty work, and freeing you from guilt."

"No!"

Before Bugz could even tell what had happened next, her screen filled with words: "You have been eliminated by Waawaate-iban. You cannot respawn at this time."

CHAPTER 30

In her dream, Bugz stepped forward into the Sundance circle. The arbor was just as she'd seen it in a nightmare more than a year prior, around when Waawaate first got sick. She seemed to float past the burning cedar at the western gate, the smoke washing over her as she entered the arena. Straight ahead, she saw tiny tobacco ties, hundreds of them in different colors, wrapped around the trunk of the tree. A mound of sage was strewn about the base of it, where the tree's trunk plunged into the earth. As she had the feeling of being carried forward, Bugz noticed the cloudy sky casting everything in an eerie light. The colors of the Sundancers around her were muted, and the sound of the singers at the big drum was distant and muffled.

Lifting her gaze up the tree, Bugz saw there were no leaves left on the branches of this monstrous cottonwood, as there would've been in a real ceremony. Instead, these limbs were barren. They resembled tortured, twisted arms clawing at the sky.

Bugz returned her gaze to eye level and felt a buffalo robe beneath her feet. She scrunched her toes in the rough welcoming fur and felt warmth. She shuddered as she recalled that the buffalo robe was only brought out to the tree when the piercing ceremony was about to begin. As she continued to wiggle her toes beneath her, Bugz felt the fur turn coarser and rougher. Before she could look down, she became aware of a presence by her side. Without looking, Bugz knew who it was—she'd been here before. She looked to her arms to check if this was in fact the same dream.

On each of her arms, just below her shoulder, a dab of ocher formed a small circle. Bugz had been marked for piercing. This piercing ceremony is as intense as any Indigenous tradition she'd known. While she'd seen her dad do it many times before, she'd never participated in it. She wanted to run away.

Turning to her left, she saw the one who she knew would cut her . . . Waawaate. She'd dreamed this before; however, in those earlier visions, her brother had always stopped short of actually trying to pierce her skin. Now he reached forward without hesitation and pinched a piece of her flesh between his thumb and forefinger. With his free hand, he raised a surgical scalpel to the heavens.

Bugz's desire to flee exploded into a debilitating terror. She could neither flee, nor move, nor scream. She was frozen and helpless to tell her brother to stop. She was trapped in a nightmare, which was just like real life.

Bugz looked up from the scalpel to what she assumed would be her brother's face. Instead, she found his mouth twisted into a crooked half-smile, the left side of his face curling up through his cheek and causing him to squint his left eye hard in the process. Finally, her lungs found her voice and she shouted loud and hard.

Still screaming, Bugz awoke in the pitch black of her bedroom. She gasped for air and didn't recognize her surroundings for a minute. Reaching for the phone on her bedside, she hesitated. She recalled the Behemoth and how he'd been terrorized by the AI. She decided not to activate the device after all.

Instead, she sprang out of bed and ran upstairs, seeking the refuge of her parents' bedroom. Her mom and dad, half-awake at best, did their best to comfort her as Bugz settled in beside them.

CHAPTER 31

Without her phone to distract her, Bugz slept late the next morning. Around noon, she found herself out of sorts as she woke in her parents' bed to the sound of her father knocking loudly on the door.

"Okay, just gimme a minute," a still-groggy Bugz grumbled from beneath her covers.

Her dad's voice came back unexpectedly firm. "No, now, Buggy. Clean yourself up and come out right away." An awkward pause reinforced the door that separated them. "Some police officers are here."

Bugz's stomach dropped and a dizzying wave of anxiety washed over her. She felt the hairs on her neck stand on end like iron filaments passed over by a magnet. "So what?" She huffed. "What does that have to—"

"Bugz," her dad said firmly. "They're here to talk to *you*."

The sound of her father's footsteps disappeared back down the hall, leaving a single question in their wake: *What do the cops want with me?*

Bugz put on her hoodie and wrapped her hair in a bun. Looking in the mirror quickly, she straightened herself out as much as possible, or as much as she could while obsessing over the police.

Walking into the living room, Bugz saw a square-jawed officer in a cowboy hat and his partner Maverick, a distant relative of her family's, who nodded to acknowledge her. His familiar face was warm, but not quite smiling. Both officers stood before Bugz, who settled beside her dad on the couch. Maverick and the cowboy sat on chairs opposite them.

"If you want to question her, I'm going to have to insist her mom is here too," Bugz's dad said.

"I appreciate your concern, Frank," Maverick began. "But this isn't questioning—there's no investigation or anything. We're just here because we figured it'd be good to"—Maverick glanced to his partner—"have a little chat." The cowboy nodded and looked out the front window.

"So, what's up?" Bugz asked softly.

"Well, games and technology aren't really my forte." Maverick scratched his tanned neck and scrunched his face slightly. "But I guess there's a problem you've created for a lot of people in a lot of places. One of your 'bots'— it's harassing and tormenting people."

Bugz sank into herself and looked to the floor as the officer explained the collateral damage of her runaway creation, reciting the mental health impacts on the other gamers, as he called them. She studied her hands and wrung them as he went on. Apparently, many family members and friends of the clanmates had demanded action against Bugz. Some of the more outspoken demanded compensation, but all agreed she had to rein in the bot.

Bugz shook her head in a sudden show of defiance, but instantly felt ashamed again when Maverick revealed that one of the other players had recently checked into a healthcare facility. "He hadn't slept in days." Maverick referred to his phone for some details. "We didn't see this person for ourselves, because he lives on the coast. But apparently he's in pretty rough shape."

"The Behemoth." Bugz cleared her throat as she thought back to the video call he'd made to Feng after the party.

Maverick glanced at his partner, who was still studying the front lawn, and then back to his phone. "Yeah, it looks like that's his alias."

"So, Buggy," her father spoke up. "Can you just call the bot off and make this go away?"

Bugz shot her father an angry look. "No, I can't." She scanned the faces of the men in the room, who all looked at her expectantly. Even the cowboy had now decided to give her his full attention. "I mean, first off, those guys aren't some innocent little gamers. They're evil." Maverick began tapping notes on his phone. Bugz continued. "Did they tell you they came here? To the Rez? They were the ones who destroyed the Thunderbird's Nest." Maverick stared at her blankly. "What?" Bugz nodded to his phone. "Aren't you going to type that into your little notepad?"

Maverick pocketed his phone, looked again to his partner, and turned back to Bugz in a way that was neither threatening nor friendly, only serious. "Bugz, listen. Right now, we're not saying you have any legal trouble, but just think it through. If this does become a problem . . . everything in the Floraverse is tracked. It would be an open-and-shut case if someone decided to pursue it."

"It's not my fault," Bugz said too quickly. She felt herself starting to sweat. "Even if I wanted to call him off, I couldn't—he's not in my control anymore. He went rogue. Honest, I can't stop him."

Maverick seemed genuinely curious. His partner looked back out the window. A group of kids rode by on bikes.

Bugz spoke again. "I don't know why you're trying to threaten me with this. I'm not responsible."

"Well, that's part of why this is so complicated." Maverick's tone offered a concession, and a slight musical tone overtook his speech as he continued, as though he were trying to signal to Bugz that he understood her predicament. "I mean, you're not harassing these people directly . . . we get that. But you created something in the digital world that's now doing things that amount to cyberbullying."

Bugz scoffed and shook her head. She bit her lower lip, hoping it would ease her frustration. "I told you guys already." They all sat in silence until Bugz could handle it no more and spoke again. "I'm not responsible," she said with finality.

"Well, then who is?" The cowboy's drawl blunted some of the curtness in his words, which were clearly more of a statement than a question. Bugz looked away from him. He continued. "Seriously, think about it." His accent wasn't from around here, though he appeared Indigenous. *He must be from down south,* Bugz thought to herself as he continued. "There's a sequence of events in motion right now that is hurting people. Damaging them. You set that sequence of events in motion. So who is responsible?" As the cowboy examined Bugz for a response, she forced herself to stare back at him, even though she wanted to stand and run. He shrugged, underlining his point, and looked back out the window.

"Okay." Frank stood. "That's enough for now. We've got some things to discuss." The officers nodded and stood quickly. They followed Frank to the door, where he showed them out with a couple of pleasantries and elbow bumps.

Bugz watched her father come back to her with an apologetic look on her face. "Sorry about that, Buggy."

He sat heavily on the couch and sighed loudly. "For what it's worth, I've got your back."

Bugz sniffed. She didn't know why she felt as she did or how to articulate it. But she wanted to cry. She brought her hoodie sleeve to her mouth and sniffed again. She shook her head.

"Thanks, Dad," Bugz said. "But they're right. It *is* my fault." She paused as she struggled to compose herself. "And I've got to do something about it."

CHAPTER 32

Deep in the woods, her face illuminated by a brilliant full moon, Bugz studied the clearing where the Thunderbird's Nest once stood. Though the monument had been desecrated and no longer held its sacred form, the power was still there—Bugz had felt it in the way her spirit swelled when she'd arrived.

Bugz raised her phone and it bathed her face in an orange glow. The energy in this place was still unlike anything else in the Floraverse and it completely overpowered her device. All that could be seen on the display was a coursing, radiating light.

Breathing deeply, Bugz prepared to respawn her 'Versona. She slipped her phone into her headset and slid it on. She knew she had but a fraction of a second between when she activated her 'Versona in AR mode and when she'd have to take control of it in the Spirit World. If she wasn't quick enough to get her 'Versona out of harm's way, the Waawaate-bot would make short work of her.

Bugz inhaled deeply again and blew this breath out slowly, so that it reminded her of a gentle breeze blowing prairie grass. She looked up to the moon and hoped for inspiration, ignoring the moon-related trivia that her virtual assistant tried to offer her in augmented reality.

"Here we go," Bugz said to herself. The neural-link in her headset detected her intent to respawn, and her viewfinder sparkled and replaced the AR scene in front of her with the completely virtual underwater scene of the buried Mishi-pizhiw nest at the bottom of Lake of the Torches.

Bugz barely had time to register the dark-green striations dimly running across the black stones that made up the lake bed before the words appeared on her screen: "You have been eliminated by Waawaate-iban. You cannot respawn at this time."

Bugz switched off the Spirit World and the augmented reality scene sprang back to life on her phone as she removed her headset. She wiped her face with her free hand, looked to the moon, and let out a short, loud yell. Her voice echoed across the clearing.

Bugz had been here for more than an hour, trying to respawn over and over again. And every single time she'd tried, she'd instantly been eliminated from the Spirit World by the Waawaate-bot. She felt discouraged, and wanted to fling her phone deep into the darkness around her, when suddenly the screen sprang to life. Feng was video-calling her. Her face softened a bit.

Bugz swiped to answer. "Hello?"

"Hey." Feng's eyebrows were raised. He appeared to take in her appearance for a second before asking, "What's the matter?"

"Nothing, I'm fine—just out here trying to get back in the Spirit World and the bot keeps killing me. He's puppy guarding!"

"Sorry, I think my automatic translator must be broken. It sounded like you said 'puppy guarding.'" Feng looked confused.

"Yeah, that's what we used to call it when we played hide-and-go-seek or grounders and someone would guard home base—just staying in one spot to tag you." Bugz felt herself relax with these childhood memories. "It wasn't very fun."

"Oh." Feng chuckled. "Weird. Never heard that before."

"What's up?"

"It's my parents . . . another video." Bugz's expression must've shown how puzzled she felt, because Feng immediately clarified. "Another video . . . and this time, they sent it to *me*."

CHAPTER 33

Feng opened the front door of his house and found Bugz standing on his doorstep out of breath. He felt a rush as he realized she'd run the entire way to his home from the Thunderbird's Nest. It felt good to know he meant something to her. He turned and led Bugz to the living room and sat on the couch. She sat immediately beside him, moving a throw pillow to sidle closer. Feng gave her a quick glance, then focused on the task at hand. He produced his phone and swiped the screen.

"I haven't watched it yet," Feng said, breathing in deeply. "I don't know if I'm ready. But I wanted you here." Bugz nodded thoughtfully. Feng found the latest video of his parents.

The video was paused on the first frame. It showed a close-up of a man in nondescript clothing with a clean-shaven face.

"Whoa," Bugz said softly, leaning even closer to Feng to study the screen. "You look like your dad." Feng felt her study his reaction before she continued. "I mean, that has to be your dad, right?"

Feng nodded. "I've never seen him without a beard before." He pressed play.

Feng's father began speaking in Mandarin. Feng swiped down through a menu and then swiped it back up. Instantly, the automatic translator kicked in mid-sentence.

"—thinking of you, son," were the first words the phone produced in English. "We have thought of you every single day. We hope you are eating well and are happy. We hope you are going to a good school and are working hard and have friends your age. We know my little sister is taking good care of you, but Farouq . . ."

Feng's dad grew silent as he looked to his feet. Feng felt the power of this moment in the space between his father's words.

Feng's dad looked up to the camera again, thick eyebrows raised to his widow's peak. "Farouq, you don't know how much we've missed you . . . our only son." He now glanced to his side, as though checking over his shoulder. "We prayed for you. Now we hope we can see you again."

Feng felt Bugz's hand on his shoulder. She rubbed his back softly. He breathed deeply, feeling the back of his ribcage expand into Bugz's caress. The sound of someone fumbling with the video recording device accompanied the jerky footage, which alternated between a set of hands, a fluorescent light, and another set of hands before turning dark.

When the image returned, it revealed a beautiful woman of middle age, Feng's mother. Her dark brown eyes were wet. She moved her lips once—a false start, as though she couldn't find the words, and then she spoke clearly. "Farouq. My baby."

Feng paused the video. He felt his body shake a few times in quick succession. He shut his eyes to try to trap the tears he felt welling up inside. He drew in a deep breath and shuddered again as he exhaled. Bugz wrapped him in an embrace. He lowered his head slowly and whispered to the phone. "Mom."

Feng shook his head slowly a half-dozen times before exhaling with a staccato sigh. He turned to Bugz, who still held him in her arms. He pressed his face into the shoulder of her hoodie. "It's been so long . . ." Bugz simply hugged him and she held him there for what felt like a really long time.

After some gentle encouragement from Bugz, Feng wiped his eyes and cleared his throat. He raised his phone and pressed play.

"It's been so long." Feng's mother echoed his thoughts. "But we never stopped thinking of you, and dreaming of the day when we could see you again. And now we can . . . Uncle found us and thinks he can get us a permit. We think we can come to you." On screen, she wiped a tear from her cheek. "We can be a family again." The video froze on a frame, as though she'd been about to say something else but was cut off.

Feng and Bugz sat together quietly. A crow cawed outside the living room window, interrupting their silent vigil. Bugz stood and walked to the glass to study the bird, scaring it from its perch in a nearby poplar tree in the process. Feng studied her as she hugged herself, rubbing the arms of her hoodie. Her features were bathed in the soft light of the moon. "That's amazing. What a gift," she said.

All Feng could do was nod as he swiped the playback back and forth on the video. With each swipe of his hand, he watched his mother wipe the tear from her face and then place it back on the spot where it had fallen.

CHAPTER 34

Bugz walked into her house, kicked off her shoes, and glanced at her mother and father, who were snuggled up in front of the TV in the living room. They smiled at her and asked about her night before returning their attention to the superhero movie they were watching. She pulled her hoodie up and made her way downstairs to her room.

As she changed clothes, Bugz thought of the northern lights she'd seen on her walk home from Feng's and what they represented. Her people, the Anishinaabe, believed the aurora represented the ancestors dancing in the Happy Hunting Grounds. She sat on the edge of her bed and put on a pair of beaded moccasins she liked to wear around the house. Bugz thought of her brother and wondered whether he was really still out there somewhere, dancing in the sky or traveling to the Spirit World.

She considered the alternative possibility—that once your life ended in this world, everything simply cut to black. She flicked off the light switch and sent her room into darkness.

Bugz thought about Feng and the breakthrough he'd experienced in receiving that video. The possibility it represented for him to someday be reunited with family. Alone with her thoughts in the dark, she recognized that she felt something else—jealousy. *Why does he get to see the people he misses again?* Bugz asked herself. *What about me?*

Shuffling in her moccasins down a path she knew from memory, Bugz found the edge of her bed. She slid across the mattress and sat up against the headboard, pulling the covers over her legs in the process. Still in pitch-black surroundings, Bugz fumbled for her phone in her hoodie pocket and retrieved it.

In the split second in which she unlocked and activated it, Bugz raised the device up to eye level in a classic bedtime reading position. As the phone sprang to life, it launched AR mode.

Immediately, crooked fangs twisted into a wide grin as the demonic Waawaate-bot flashed on screen. The terrifying specter stood at the foot of Bugz's bed, glowing infrared in the darkness. Before she could react, the bot lunged forward and scurried on all fours across the mattress with the speed of a striking alligator. In an instant, the bot snapped its jaws open wider and bared row upon row of sharpened teeth, a ravenous shark set to devour her. The speed at which the attack unfolded was inhuman, the contortion of the bot's joints and jaw beyond anything possible in the natural world.

In sheer terror, Bugz threw her phone at where she pictured the attacking ghoul to be and sprang to her feet. She flipped the light switch on immediately and screamed, before she regained her senses and told herself the ghoul could not physically harm her. As she silently repeated this mantra, it dawned on her that psychological harm was another matter entirely—she knew she'd never be able to sleep in her room that night after what she'd seen.

Bugz grabbed her phone, flung the door open, and ran upstairs to her parents. They greeted her at the top of the stairs, asking what was the matter. "It's that bot. The one the cops were here about."

It was clear from their expressions that they didn't understand what she meant, and after making sure that Bugz hadn't been physically hurt, they moved back to the living room. Bugz settled in near them beneath a blanket to watch the rest of the movie, doing her best to shake the terrifying image of the contorted, desecrated version of her brother's face lashing out at her.

CHAPTER 35

The outboard motor roared as Bugz maneuvered the aluminum boat away from the Rez and deeper into the lake. The wind of this unseasonably cool day felt good against Bugz's face, even as it brought with it the occasional spray of water. She studied Feng, who faced forward watching the scenery fly by. Islands covered in jack pine and cedar rose and fell beside them, each soaked with water stains earned over the centuries.

Bugz closed her eyes and saw him in her mind's eye, the ghoulish twin of her brother lunging at her with his snarled fangs. She opened her eyes and shook her head. This is how it had been for the past number of days—Bugz had been hounded by the evil Waawaate-bot wherever she went, to the point where she couldn't use her phone anymore. School, home, the Thunderbird's Nest—no matter where she was, he was there waiting for her. Anytime she turned her device on, he leapt forward, tormenting her with his now unrecognizable face. What had begun as a simple upturned smile had now morphed into a demonic grin cranked impossibly high to one side in a way that a real living being could never sustain. For some reason, his appearance had also taken on the appearance of death and decay. Bugz didn't understand why this had happened to her virtual creation, but she shook her head as she allowed that it fit the bot's current state quite accurately. He was the undead, pursuing her beyond all reason and past any human limit. Now he was even haunting her outside of the 'Verse, living rent free in her head and appearing in her thoughts any time she closed her eyes.

Feng turned to her and smiled, unable to speak over the roar of the motor and wind. Bugz forced a smile back.

After banking around a few islands and into a channel, Bugz throttled the motor down expertly so that the boat slowed smoothly and maintained just enough momentum to coast to the shore.

Bugz watched Feng tie a sailor's knot and then cast her gaze up to the massive rock face before them. In ocher paint set against the midnight-blue stone, she could see their destination—the Everlasting Road.

She trudged up the mossy incline, grabbing a tree every now and again like a handrail to steady herself. The angle was steep but Bugz knew her way around environments like this one—she'd spent as much time in the bush as anyone else her age. Arriving at the ledge beneath the giant rock painting, she turned back to check on Feng, who was only a few steps behind her. He joined her on this scaffold, placed his hands on his hips, and turned his head to the sky, searching for his breath.

"So, what now?" he asked, looking at Bugz.

Bugz shook her head and considered this. She realized she didn't have a good answer. "I can't really explain . . ." She took her phone out of her pocket and spun it in her hand, delaying the moment when she'd find out whether or not the Waawaate-bot had pursued her here too.

"Well, your stupid bot has made it impossible for either of us to use our phones anywhere. Worth a shot, right?" Feng withdrew his phone as well. "I mean, I'd like to be able to send a message back to my parents."

Bugz bit her lip and looked up at the rock painting. "I'm really sorry."

"It's not your fault."

Bugz looked to Feng, searching. She really hoped he meant it, but couldn't read his expression. She tried to explain her theory. "I just feel like this place is the last spot where maybe there's some magic left, or where we've got a chance to hide from him for a little while."

"No time like the present."

"Right." Bugz put on her headset, snapped her phone into place, and looked to Feng again for reassurance. He was already putting his headset on, but seemed to sense her gaze. He snapped his phone into the headset and then stopped, awaiting her move.

Bugz stepped closer and stared deeply into Feng's eyes. She studied the overlapping textures, the shades of amber and bronze. Bugz smiled as she remembered the first time they'd locked eyes in their homeroom class a year ago. She recalled thinking of the far reaches of the universe, and how she'd felt about him from the first time she'd seen him. She planted a kiss on his cheek.

Her smile broadened as she spoke again. "Let's go then."

"'Skoden,'" he replied.

CHAPTER 36

It happened so quickly Feng barely had a chance to witness it, much less process what occurred.

It took place the moment he launched into the 'Verse.

As his headset sprang to life and laid an augmented reality version of the scene around him—rock painting, rock face, moss-covered ledge—his heart sank. For some reason, he couldn't see Bugz, even though she should've been right next to him. Instead, the first thing he saw was the Waawaate-bot crouched like a jungle cat ready to spring on his prey. The bot's fangs were glistening, and dripping virtual saliva. Yet the bot wasn't prepared to attack Feng; instead, his body was angled slightly off-center, as though he'd just lined Bugz up in his sights and then she'd disappeared, surprising him.

Immediately, still within the first second of Feng entering AR mode and before he could react, the bot reset and spun to face him with sickening speed. The bot moved with such quickness that he sprang from his ready position and flung his jaws wide open before Feng could even raise his arms to shield himself. Just as quickly, the bot was upon him and Feng could see the sky above. The sun shone brilliantly.

Feng struggled to fight off the bot, and yet he felt strangely calm. Nothing further was happening to eliminate him from the 'Verse, as had been the case for days prior.

Instead, a ray of sunlight caught his eye and appeared to flare through his headset. In this beam, he saw a one-dimensional image of Bugz reaching for him. Before he could reach back to her, he felt her pulling him with a violent force.

Feng swore that he'd just had his spirit pulled from his body. Vertigo, motion sickness, dizziness . . . these terms all failed to capture the disorientation Feng felt as he was dragged behind Bugz into another realm.

A sudden flash of pure bright light relieved him of this pain.

As the light receded and left Feng squinting, he tried to make sense of what he'd just seen. Everything, from the bot attack to being saved by Bugz to the tilt-o-whirl feeling, had happened in less than the time it took him to raise his hand and snap his fingers.

While Feng didn't understand the scene he'd just witnessed, he realized that Bugz's hunch had been right—

the rock painting had allowed them to escape the bot.

As the light dimmed further and Feng could begin to make out what lay before him, he found himself face-to-face with Bugz, who was within arm's reach.

"Don't move," she said. "And don't look down."

Predictably, Feng looked down.

A different sickness overcame him—a fear of heights. He saw that he and Bugz were standing on a white beam no wider than a bus bench.

Below was nothing but darkness, though Feng could sense this was a drop that terminated hundreds of stories below.

Feng closed his eyes and felt Bugz's grip steady him on either side.

He could hear her smiling through her voice as she spoke again. "Told you not to look."

CHAPTER 37

Bugz walked slowly and deliberately with her arms out-stretched, as though crossing a tightrope. The white beam was considerably larger than the cables she'd seen dare-devils use in videos she'd watched before, but the distance below was also much deeper than any span they'd dared traverse. The bottom of this floor was so far away that light could not reach it. *Don't fall*, she told herself.

Bugz felt the beam begin to vibrate beneath her feet. The pulses weren't regular, like a drum beat, but they weren't totally random either. She thought of an animal crossing a frozen lake. Squinting into the distance, she could see a form far ahead of them. It appeared blurry at first. As the pulses grew stronger and the figure grew closer, Bugz leaned in. She recognized the being.

"Sabikeshiinh," she whispered, just loud enough for Feng to hear.

"Care to translate?"

"Spider." Bugz focused intensely. "That was my first word in Ojibwe. When I was a baby." She looked back to Feng and then forward again. "I just can't tell if this thing is friend or foe."

"Does it change anything? I mean, we can't really run . . ." Feng seemed to consider his words. "Or fight. At least not effectively."

The vibrations rocking the beam began to increase with such an intensity that Bugz and Feng were forced to lower themselves and hang on to keep from falling off. The massive spider rushed toward them. They braced for an attack as the beam shook violently.

At the last moment, the spider stopped. Calm returned as the vibrations dissipated down the plank. Looking up, Bugz could see the arachnid stood more than twice her height. Two sets of jet-black eyes that seemed to see right through her. The dark orbs moved slightly as they studied her. She felt as though the being knew she was afraid. Sabikeshiinh turned ninety degrees and shot a gleaming material forward a distance too far for Bugz to see. The material seemed to land somewhere unseen as it solidified into a beam much like the one Bugz was already standing on. The spider connected this new plank to the current one and began walking away on this new ninety-degree angle.

Bugz and Feng looked to one another, shrugged their shoulders, and followed the spider down its new path. They kept a safe distance to minimize the vibrations, but were also careful not to fall too far behind. They kept silent for a long time until finally Feng spoke up.

"Where are we?"

"I have no idea," Bugz said, whispering in an attempt to try and get Feng to follow suit. "We're obviously not in AR. But we're not in the Spirit World either."

"How do you know?"

"Well, for one, I've never seen this place before." Bugz realized this wasn't a strong argument. "And two, I don't seem to have 'my powers.'" She made air quotes as she spoke. "I can't fly, I can't summon anything to my side, I can't even see what lies ahead." She thought about this for a moment. "I guess I'm just normal."

"Don't sound so crushed." Bugz turned to see Feng grin.

After what seemed like an eternity on this tightrope, the spider stopped and turned to its left. They'd arrived at an intersection with another beam.

"Hey! Where are we?" Feng shouted to the spider. There was no reaction as the giant arachnid trudged along its new path. "You try." Feng nudged Bugz.

"Hey, spider . . ." Bugz felt ridiculous as she started speaking, but even more so when the giant arachnid ignored her and continued on its course. Bugz looked to Feng for help.

"I dunno, try your language," Feng offered.

"Okay." Bugz somehow felt more self-conscious. She knew it wouldn't work—it was a silly idea. She cleared her throat. "Hey, Sabikeshiinh."

The huge spider stopped in his path. The beam's vibrations settled. Bugz shot Feng a surprised look and turned back to the arachnid.

"Where are we?"

The spider remained silent. After an awkward pause, Sabikeshiinh turned back and walked right up to Bugz and Feng. Looking over their heads, the spider cast a beam of light back toward the intersection from which they'd just come. Bugz turned and saw a beautiful young woman with blonde hair in a fashion-forward outfit floating in the air. She looked two-dimensional, as though projected onto a screen hovering above the intersection.

"What is it?" Bugz asked.

"It's someone's 'Versona. It's off-the-rack, for sure. I've seen it before."

"'Course you've seen her before."

The spider turned and projected another beam of light toward the first intersection they'd crossed. After a moment, a second screen came zooming out of the distance and flew toward Bugz. As it did, a young man wearing a kaffiyeh and baseball hat was visible on it. Bugz pondered the image. "Another 'Versona, I guess." She looked back to Feng. "Still doesn't tell us where we are."

At this, the spider shot an innumerable number of beams of light in the 360 degrees that surrounded them horizontally. The beams of light flashed and pulsed. Soon, the beams were drawing hundreds, then thousands of screens near, each projecting the image of a different 'Versona. The beams of light and the 'Versonas they displayed continued multiplying as more and more drew closer to Bugz and Feng. They featured tremendous diversity, representing every conceivable shade of skin—including some alien hues, every style of dress, and numerous mods for battle and sport. Bugz recognized some of the 'Versonas as they drew nearer. She recognized Stormy's friend Chalice on one screen. The Amazonian frame of a fan who'd bought an ax from her in the past appeared on another. Bugz even saw Alpha on one of them—she recognized his frightened expression. His 'Versona was still frozen in the Waawaate-bot's icy lair.

"This is amazing," Feng said. "There must be billions of 'Versonas in here. It's like your spider friend has every 'Versona in the world."

Bugz thought about this for a second. "We're in the center of the Floraverse."

Suddenly, the billions of screens with their billions of 'Versonas evaporated, as did the rays of light projecting them. The giant spider turned and began trudging back down the beam.

"Guess you were right," Feng offered. "He's not much for words, but he's powerful."

"How do you know it's a him?"

"Fair. *They* are very powerful."

The couple marched along after the spider for a hundred steps before Bugz tested her luck again.

"Sabikeshiinh." The spider stopped. "I've always wondered about the engine that powers the Floraverse. Like, if we're all processing the 'Verse on our phones, and connecting with each other along the way . . . there's something connecting everyone online. The blockchain." Sabikeshiinh remained motionless. "You're part of that?"

The spider resumed walking.

Bugz looked to Feng with an excited expression on her face. "And Sabikeshiinh." The spider came to a halt. "I've always wondered who put the respawn point in the Thunderbird's Nest. That was you, right?" The spider began moving again.

Through this trial-and-error question period, painstaking as it was, Bugz managed to gain a clearer sense of what was taking place. The spider wasn't really a spider at all—it was an algorithm that forged a consensus across the blockchain of the Floraverse, helping to link each player together and allowing them to interact with others. It was representing itself as a spider to allow Bugz and Feng to visualize it. The spider's web was another visualization, representing the blockchain connecting all the users of the Floraverse to one another. Feng and Bugz were in neither the Spirit World nor in AR . . . they were in the framework of the 'Verse itself, watching the algorithm build and maintain the infrastructure of their virtual world.

The spider plodded forward on its latest path. Feng spoke from behind Bugz. "Sabikeshiinh." The spider stopped again. "So, is the reason there are Anishinaabe symbols all over the 'Verse—like the Thunderbird's Nest, the Everlasting Road, the northern lights—because Bugz, the best player in the game, is Anishinaabe, and you wanted to send her signals so you could lead her in certain directions . . ." Feng glanced to Bugz before continuing. "But if she was Chinese or French or Igbo, you would've built the Floraverse around symbols from those cultures instead?" The spider remained motionless.

"What?" Feng asked. "I thought for sure that was the explanation."

Bugz smirked. "Maybe Sabikeshiinh's just annoyed by your long, run-on sentence of a question." The spider began marching again. Bugz chuckled.

"Remember after Clan:LESS destroyed the Thunderbird's Nest, but the magic still came back?" Feng whispered to Bugz as they began moving again. "I told you then that it was you. I still believe that. I'll still prove it to you somehow."

Bugz shook her head and blushed almost imperceptibly. She closed her eyes for a moment, embarrassed at the idea of having the 'Verse built around her.

Before she could speak again, a bolt of lightning crashed into the beam and sent Feng flying toward the abyss. Bugz jumped and grabbed him by the arm, saving him from plunging into the virtual nothingness. Without looking, she reached back and grabbed the beam with her free hand. She clutched it with a death grip. Grimacing with effort, she wondered to herself how much Feng weighed. Bugz groaned as the beam began reverberating violently, loosening her grip in the process.

A commotion caught her eye. She looked above and saw the spider lunging back and forth, grappling with an unseen force on the other side. Sabikeshiinh was spinning web after web in front of itself. Just as quickly as it did, a bolt of lightning would crash and destroy the material that'd been spun. The giant spider threw a few webs at a higher angle, apparently attempting to trap its target.

The spider leapt forward at its tormentor. As it did, the Waawaate-bot flew quickly into view, firing lightning bolts at the spider below. The bot circled above and locked eyes with Bugz. His crooked smile widened and revealed sharp fangs covered in plaque. The bot dove forward with great speed, collaring Bugz and Feng in each of his arms. With their necks secured, he shot straight up toward a brilliant light that shone far above them.

The Waawaate-bot hurdled ahead with such speed that the plank on which Bugz had just hung shrank quickly into the distance. It grew smaller and smaller until the beam appeared no thicker than a thread. From this vantage point, Bugz could finally see the spider's web for what it was . . . the countless beams intersected with one another in a beautiful concentric spiral pattern that spun out from a central, circular void.

A Dreamcatcher.

Bugz had no time to appreciate its beauty. As she looked up to the light again, she felt her stomach drop. She was all but certain the bot was dragging them back to the Spirit World, where he could eliminate them.

Bugz fought hard and ripped violently at the bot's grip, but it had no effect. They kept rocketing skyward.

Suddenly, inertia struck her and Feng with a tremendous force, stopping them in their tracks. It felt like being body-checked. The bot fought furiously to keep pulling them higher. Yet no matter how hard the AI struggled, the trio began to lose altitude. Bugz looked down and saw a long, gleaming, sinewy line leading back to the Dreamcatcher below, like a fiber optic strand. Sabikeshiinh had caught them. Another shining thread came speeding toward them. The bot had to release his grip in order to dodge it. When he did, gravity pulled Bugz and Feng down quickly. She saw a look of hesitation on the bot's crooked face—he was debating whether to swoop back down at them. Instead, the bot shot up and into the light.

Accelerating back down toward the spider's web, trapped in Sabikeshiinh's embrace, Bugz turned to Feng and smiled.

"They say Dreamcatchers keep the nightmares away."

CHAPTER 38

Moonlight illuminated the Everlasting Road and the rock face on which it was painted. Removing her headset, Bugz ran her hands through her hair and led Feng back down through the darkness and to the shore.

Bugz untied the sailor's knot in one smooth motion as Feng's phone provided a flashlight by which she could launch their watercraft. From the corner of her eye, she could see him scrolling.

"Looks like the traitor is at it again," Feng said absentmindedly. Entranced by his screen, he continued. "She's all over the comment sections in the 'Verse, saying how you're going to get arrested for cyberbullying and causing harm to all these people through the bot." He shook his head. "She's obsessed."

Bugz felt a grimace creep across her face as she motioned for Feng to climb aboard. As he did, she pushed off the rock shore and jumped on the bow of the boat. She climbed to the back and pressed the fuel bulb furiously. She did this almost solely by feel, low as the light was. Bugz muttered, "Don't read me any more comments from her. She's just a hater." She paused when the fuel bulb felt full. "We finally find a way to escape the bot, at least for now, and she's still hating. Even when we finish dealing with him, she'll probably still try to cancel me anyway." Bugz launched the boat and continued muttering to herself. "In the future, everyone will be canceled for fifteen minutes." She shook her head as she recognized her self-pity.

The noise of the boat motor overtook the sound of everything else around them, leaving Bugz to wonder why the traitor had such power over her. She couldn't stop thinking about her. She'd even changed her 'Versona's appearance because of the way the traitor made her feel. Bugz shook her head. She placed her phone in her lap and opened a window that showed her 'Versona. She tweaked the skin back to the way she looked in real life. She ditched the 'Versona's bodysuit for her black hoodie. She scrunched her face at the image of herself on the device. Bugz gave the virtual version of herself long hair again, the way it had been before Waawaate's funeral. She shut the window and pocketed her phone.

The black water broke into small peaks every few feet as the wind blew waves around them. The boat leapt over these small inclines as the moon touched each with light, tracing a bright path through the darkness. Bugz closed her eyes to focus on the feel of the wind on her face. She didn't need sight to make it home—her parents had led her across these waters since she'd been in utero. She'd made this trek in sun and in rain, in light and in dark, in summer and in winter, by boat and by truck. She could make it the whole way home strictly by feel. Perhaps this is what it meant to be Indigenous, to be Anishinaabe. Bugz decided that, at the very least, this is what it meant to belong. She sighed.

Bugz heard Feng's voice, but couldn't make out the words. She opened her eyes and found him waving his phone at her, its screen blinding her with light. It was ringing with a video call from a caller whose name was represented with Chinese calligraphy.

"What?" Bugz mouthed to Feng.

Feng shouted again, but Bugz shook her head; she couldn't hear a thing. She watched him draw a deep breath and shout again. "It's my uncle!"

Bugz throttled the boat down as quickly as she could without sending them overboard. "Answer it!"

CHAPTER 39

"Hello?" Feng didn't like how nervous he sounded as he rushed to answer, but he couldn't stop himself. "Hello? Hello? Hello?"

The screen on his phone locked in the video feed and revealed his mother, looking as she had in the previous video—aged, weary, skinny. Yet seeing her face stirred something in Feng . . . it was the first face Feng had learned to love. It was the first face he'd ever seen. For all that her features testified she'd been through in the years since Feng had seen her last, his mother's eyes were still dark and young and full of life, reflecting a curved version of whatever fluorescence hung above her. She appeared concerned, though it must have been only for the quality of their connection. In an instant, her expression softened and a smile spread from cheek to cheek.

"Farouq!" she exclaimed. "My baby!"

Feng found tears in his eyes, but could not find words to match the feeling in his heart.

"Farouq, my baby, it's so good to see you again." She looked to her right and said something inaudible. As she turned her device, Feng saw his father leaning into the frame.

"Farouq!" His father's face broke into a wide grin. "Look at you, my boy, you're almost a man!" He repeated this to Feng's mother and looked expectantly back at the screen. "It's been a long time, son."

Finally, Feng found words. "Mom, Dad, it's so good to see you. How are you? How have you been?"

"Now that we see you, we are good," Feng's mother said with tears in her eyes.

"What have we been doing, son? We've been dreaming of this moment every night, and praying for it every day. The moment we finally see you again." Feng's father could not stop smiling.

Feng's mind raced with questions. The shame and anger he'd felt for so many years rushed to the surface. Experiencing these feelings again . . . staring at the image of his parents, he saw the beliefs that triggered those emotions didn't matter anymore, so he let them go. All he could think to ask were simple questions about where they lived and how they were sustaining themselves. Their answers matched the broad strokes that his auntie Liumei had shared with him.

Finally, his dad spoke with his typical directness.

"Farouq, we can't speak much longer. The party doesn't let us have phones here—we're using your uncle's. This is the first call we've made in years, and it was to you. I hope you know how much you mean to us."

"When can I speak to you again?" Feng asked.

His mother interrupted his father, who'd looked set to speak. "Farouq, my baby, we are going to come to you. Uncle is making the arrangements now. We hope to follow your tracks through Turkey and then to North America."

"Son, understand this," his father jumped in. "We made a promise when they dragged us out of our home so many years ago. It's a promise we made to each other time and time again. Through the detention and the torture. It's a promise we renewed right before we made this call. We promised, no matter what it took and no matter what the cost, we were going to find you and make sure that we could be together again."

Feng smiled through tears. He sniffed as he felt them trace warm paths down his cheeks. He wiped his eyes before his mother spoke again.

"We are going to be reunited as a family, Farouq. We are going to come to you. We love you. But we have to go now." She paused to draw a deep breath. "Let this carry you until we see you again—the next time we speak, we will be speaking in person. Face-to-face, and heart-to-heart."

Feng nodded as his parents each told him again how much they loved him.

The call terminated on their end, leaving Feng in darkness, the slow rocking motion of the boat left to soothe him as the sound of the idling motor droned on. Feng took a moment to compose himself before looking back to the stern of the boat. There, his eyes found Bugz smiling through tears of her own.

The midnight-black waves stretched behind her into infinity.

CHAPTER 40

Waawaate, the real Waawaate, took a step forward, his beautiful moccasins touching down silently on the starry road on which he traveled. As he propelled himself forward, Waawaate no longer marveled at the supernovae that burst around him or the nebulae that stretched their wings like butterflies, ejecting colors in all directions. He looked down to the trail of stardust on which he walked, only to look past it and focus on the infinite black distance beyond. Loneliness wrapped itself around him.

Waawaate could not remember how long he'd been walking. When he tried to think of his loved ones, he could not picture them. He could still name them, though: Mom. Dad. Bugz. Stormy.

Stormy. At this, his mind's eye flashed an image of the terrifying sight he'd encountered earlier on this path. He thought of the log that had been something like a snake, and the debris that crashed ashore downstream. He looked around and studied the infinite expanse of space, stars, and the astral plains surrounding him. He realized his situation. Though he didn't know how he'd arrived at this place, he knew where he was. He couldn't remember how it had transpired, but in this moment, he understood what had happened to him.

Waawaate reached into his pocket, retrieved some tobacco, and placed it down on the path in front of him. Crouching with his eyes closed, Waawaate began to pray. He asked the spirits to care for his relatives who were surely suffering now. Waawaate felt so bad for the family he knew he'd left behind; guilty, even. As he prayed, the gruff voice of the Elder came to him.

There should be a strawberry just up ahead, just a little farther on this path.

Waawaate stood and brushed the last bits of tobacco from his hand. He thought he heard an echo in the distance. He couldn't be sure, but it sounded human.

He walked for so long that he grew bored, yet Waawaate knew he had to continue moving forward . . . so he counted his steps. After counting more than a hundred thousand, and after feeling increasingly sorry for himself over the last ninety-nine thousand or so, Waawaate looked down to his feet. He came to a standstill.

"There it is," Waawaate said quietly to himself as he stared at a strawberry beaded into the vamp of his moccasin. He brought his other foot in line with his first and found a second beaded strawberry. A tear escaped his eye and floated off into space.

I am not yet in those Happy Hunting Grounds, he thought to himself, *for my heart still aches. But I will know that place by its perfection.*

As he began to walk again, he realized he was at the foot of a large hill. The path climbed in elevation before him even as it remained black and starry. On either side of this trail lay tall grass, long and disheveled, as though it had grown fast but then been suddenly deprived of water. These grasses swung and swayed in a gentle breeze that Waawaate had, at least until that moment, not noticed. He stared at the slow-moving brush for a long time. Though so familiar to him in shape, this long grass had taken on a hue he'd never seen before. Some part of this color was borrowed from the nostalgic, halcyon light that can only be seen in the late afternoon of a summer's day. Some other part of this color was the black-light purple glow only seen after midnight in certain ceremonial settings.

Waawaate could not name this color, so he stared at it, mesmerized by the moving plants. When the wind picked up, he realized he could not name this color because no one could see it during their earthly existence. It could only be seen here, in this place, on this road. He wiped his eye and looked further up the path.

The strong wind blew some of the brush over to his right, and there he caught a glimpse of a strawberry bush—low to the ground like the wild strawberries back home, but much larger, and bearing leaves of an almost radioactive green. Waawaate could not resist. He stepped forward and plucked a plump, glowing, pinkish-red berry from its stem.

Waawaate brought the heart-berry to his face. He could see all the colors of the setting sun in this tiny fruit. He placed it in his mouth. *Perfection.*

Swallowing, Waawaate looked toward the summit of the giant incline. The road stretched ahead a much greater distance than he'd originally understood. The wind picked up again and beat down the tall iridescent grass. This action revealed millions of bushes of these sunset strawberries covering the hill in every conceivable direction. To his left, to his right, straight up ahead, all Waawaate could see were these plants blowing in the breeze, the tiny fruits seeming to dance on their branches.

The strawberry mountain.

In the wind, Waawaate could hear the sound of another voice. He closed his eyes and tried hard to listen. At first, nothing came. He focused more intently still; suddenly, the sound came to him like a flood. A joyous sound, a playful sound. The sound of children laughing. People laughing. Elders speaking with smiles in their voices. Many voices as one, like a symphony of pow-wow singers belting out the most beautiful, bittersweet, soulful melody. They sang in multipart harmony, their song punctuated with images of happiness and sacrifice that landed in the core of his being. Everything that ever was and ever will be was wrapped up in pure selfless love and delivered to his heart in that instant.

He opened his eyes and his vision returned to him. The strawberries danced all over the mountain. The ancestors sang to him, calling him home. His heart ached for all he'd left behind.

The Elder spoke again. *There is no looking back, only moving forward.*

Waawaate tore up the hill, sprinting along this path of stars . . . the Path of Souls.

CHAPTER 41

Bugz awoke in her room, crying. Her brother, lost and alone, sprinting up a hill of dead, drying grass. The images left her mind's eye as soon as she sniffed in the darkness and wiped her face. She reached for her phone and its brilliance blinded her.

Feng answered the video call after a few rings. His eyes puffy and barely open, he asked her what she wanted in the middle of the night.

"Let's go do it now," Bugz said firmly. "Enough running . . . let's finish it now."

She hung up the call before he could respond, snapped her phone into its headset, and plunged into the Floraverse.

CHAPTER 42

The moment Bugz entered the Realm of the Dream-catcher, the Waawaate-bot was upon her. He grabbed her by the shoulders and flung her off a beam of light and into the empty space of nothingness before she could even get her bearings straight.

By the time Bugz realized what was happening, Sabikeshiinh had already caught her in a shining strand of web and was hauling her back toward another beam, even as it fended off the swarming bot with its free arms. Their assailant looked like a mad dragonfly darting to and fro around the giant spider. Within the depths of her stomach, Bugz could feel the acceleration of the giant arachnid pulling her. She was flying at a great speed.

Before she could make it safely to the nearest light beam, her movement caught the eye of the Waawaate-bot and he charged her again, swooping in like a bird of prey. He grabbed her by the shoulders and tried to wrest her from the embrace of Sabikeshiinh's web. Bugz started hand-fighting the bot—peeling his hands loose from their grips on her and then countering his new grips when he re-established his hold on her, over and over again. She looked and noticed the effort on the spider's face as it continued trying to drag her in. The fight had caused her to veer off course from one beam and toward another, farther from Sabikeshiinh. Bugz could tell the web would soon snap, as it was growing perilously thin midway through its length. Continuing to hand-fight the Waawaate-bot, she saw another intersection of two sets of light beams grow near. Bugz pictured the player in the Floraverse who occupied this node in the blockchain and had an idea.

"Send me to that 'Versona, whoever it is!" she shouted to Sabikeshiinh. "Send me to whichever location he's at in the 'Verse!"

Instantly, the image of a 'Versona—a tall, blue, canine warrior with ancient Egyptian-like armor—flashed in front of Bugz. She tumbled from the Realm of the Dreamcatcher and into the region of the Spirit World where this 'Versona had been preparing for battle as part of his local clan. Bugz fell to the sand, ninja-rolled, and popped back up on her feet, doing her best to ignore the motion sickness the jump between worlds had caused.

"Bugz?" The giant dog soldier's expression betrayed his total surprise. "What are you doing here?" He looked to a nearby friend, also in ancient Egyptian garb, and then back to Bugz. "Are you here to help Sun-R@ clan fight the twisted one?"

Before she could confess she'd never heard of their crew, the Waawaate-bot was upon her again. He tackled her and together they rolled over and over again down the side of a tall sand dune. The bot landed on top of her and reached back toward the white sun blazing high above, preparing to deliver the blow that would finish Bugz once and for all. He plunged his fist down. Just before it crashed into Bugz, a stream of web appeared in the Spirit World and yanked Bugz violently back to the Realm of the Dreamcatcher. The feeling of vertigo that accompanied this leaping of worlds was starting to become familiar.

Shaking her head, Bugz refocused on her surroundings. She was flying above the Dreamcatcher, which shone brilliantly below her. Sabikeshiinh was trying to haul her in. Of course, the Waawaate-bot made his interdimensional appearance and flew toward her, grabbing her by the feet and pulling her from the spider's grip.

Another intersection in the web of the Dreamcatcher approached. The 'Versona of a young woman who'd adorned her face with red war paint in a style Bugz vaguely recognized as Amazonian appeared before her. Bugz nodded to the spider and was sent spiraling into this part of the Spirit World. She sprawled onto the floor of the woman's home, which looked as though it was set in a futuristic favela. Before she could stand, the bot attacked her again. And before the bot could eliminate her, Sabikeshiinh once again pulled her back to the Dreamcatcher.

And so it went. The Waawaate-bot pursued Bugz relentlessly from realm to realm as Sabikeshiinh pulled her from location to location, from Spirit World back to the Dreamcatcher and from the Dreamcatcher back to Spirit World, causing Bugz infinite confusion and dizziness but always keeping her one step ahead.

The 'Versonas she visited flashed by like visions in a fever dream: a group of celebrity-influencer clones on a massive boat partying like there was no tomorrow, each attempting the perfect selfie. An Afro-futurist collective building a massive spherical monument with flying construction equipment. A tribe of Vikings on an ice world gathering their forces. A rusted fleet of mecha-exo-skeletons marching in formation on a scorched earth. The most beautiful 'Versona she'd ever seen. The most grotesque. Bugz noticed they all shared movements that seemed to be characterized by a frantic energy. They were behaving as though they were living on borrowed time.

Whenever Bugz flashed into these far corners of the Floraverse, the 'Versonas reacted with shock and awe as the most well-known player in the game's history appeared before them. They were all stunned a second time when Bugz was set upon just as quickly by a demonic stalker and then quickly yanked away from them, disappearing into thin air.

Glancing at a giant screen in a packed e-sports stadium that she'd been transported to in one part of the Spirit World, Bugz saw she'd become a trending topic. All of the witnesses spotting her across the far reaches of the Floraverse were spreading the word. She scanned some of the top comments on the Jumbotron.

"Anubi5.555: WAR BUGZ! We see you fighting the scourge of the 'Verse! We join you in arms!"

"**Solemnity**: Bugz and the Joker who torments us, the yin and the yang, flash and disappear . . . sure signs of the apocalypse."

"KeenWahPartyPeep: Bugz sighting confirmed. And the evil one we all hate too. This is the most epic night ever!"

Bugz's heart sank as she realized what these comments meant—the Waawaate-bot had run amuck far beyond her circles and those of Clan:LESS. The entire Floraverse was now being tormented by the AI. The speed at which he could teleport combined with his insatiable drive and corrupted outlook meant he'd soon render the game unusable.

As Bugz was pulled back to the Realm of the Dreamcatcher, and while still fighting the bot, she opened a window in her heads-up display to read more comments. Over and over again she saw 'Versonas reporting that the bot was on the verge of destroying the 'Verse. That's why the warriors were preparing for battle; that's why the spiritual were in prayer and why the party people were behaving like it was their last night in the Spirit World. Unless Bugz could do something about it once and for all, it would be everyone's last night in the 'Verse. An intense guilt settled over Bugz as she imagined a Floraverse in the near future ruled only by the Waawaate-bot and rendered inhospitable to anyone else by his constant torment. All she could do was grit her teeth and keep fighting.

The Waawaate-bot closed in on her bit by bit, learning the pattern by which Sabikeshiinh transferred her from place to place with the relentless efficiency of an algorithm optimizing itself over a growing set of data. Sabikeshiinh reacted to the AI's improvement by accelerating the pace at which it flung Bugz into new locations within the Spirit World and yanked her back to the Realm of the Dreamcatcher. Through it all, Bugz felt a sickness that forced her to close her eyes tightly. She could sense her mouth watering. She clenched her teeth tighter and tighter, resolving to make it through. This was the only way to rid the 'Verse of the bot. Her greatest enemy. Her finest creation. Her dear brother.

No, she thought to herself. *He's not my brother.* Bugz opened her eyes and saw the twisted smile and sharpened fangs of the barely recognizable face as the bot wrestled her.

Amidst this chaos, Bugz gradually grew accustomed to the sickness and began to focus on defending the attacks from the Waawaate-bot. Knowing she'd not be able to strike him—he was too quick for that—she instead focused on blocking his sorties, wresting his grips from her when he did grab hold of her, and sticking up a knee or elbow to prevent him from getting too close. Soon, she found she could anticipate where he'd be coming from—typically the opposite direction from which he'd just attacked. She was learning too.

Each time Bugz entered a new realm, there was a quick flash, some code in the 'Verse's engine designed to signal to the user the change in surroundings. Yet as the world-changing grew so quick, the flashes began to drown out Bugz's surroundings until eventually they became so rapid as to appear continuous.

From this moment on, it felt to Bugz as though it were just her and the Waawaate-bot, fighting each other in a never-ending tunnel of white light. She'd fend him off from one side and he'd set upon her from another; she'd throw him over her shoulder with a judo technique in one direction and he'd drop down on her shoulders trying to pin her from another.

The battle accelerated to a fever pitch of intensity and luminosity.

CHAPTER 43

Feng logged in to the 'Verse and entered the Realm of the Dreamcatcher just as this frenzy was kicking off. Ignored by the Waawaate-bot, he ran to Sabikeshiinh and sheltered behind them for protection. From the safety of this vantage point, Feng watched the battle unfold.

Strands of web arced off into the distance, anticipating a spot where Bugz would appear, and then dragged her for the short time it took the bot to intercept her before the pair would disappear in a flash. Then they'd reappear somewhere else to start the cycle again.

The webs were soon cast off in every direction, all around, above and below Feng. He could do nothing but watch as the organized confusion, flashes of lights, and explosions of skirmish picked up speed and ferocity.

To Feng, it looked like a lightning storm in space punctuated by brief appearances from his girlfriend and the ghoulish echo of that which was once her brother. At the center of it all was the maestro, Sabikeshiinh.

Soon, Feng could not even make out the different stages of the battle unfolding around him. It was all simply happening too fast. Here, the flashes became a vividly undulating cloud of light which ebbed and flowed like waves on a sea.

Suddenly, the electrical storm hit a tipping point and the bright white lights exploded in color. Blue waves crashed into purple, then folded in on themselves and re-emerged as shimmering greens and yellows. Feng recognized he was witnessing something truly special.

The northern lights.

"Waawaate," he whispered.

CHAPTER 44

Bugz did not notice at first—the effort and concentration required to keep the Waawaate-bot at bay in an ever-quickening whirlwind of activity consumed her.

At one point, though, as she tore the bot's grip from her shin, she realized she was gradually gaining the upper hand. The next time the bot set upon her, she'd already spun around to defend, reached around his shoulder, and greeted him with a hip toss. The next direction he attacked from was below, but Bugz simply shoved her boot toward him and pushed him away. She had turned the tide and was slowly wearing the bot down, clearly damaging him in some instances. Yet the Waawaate-bot remained relentless—he seemed simply unable to abandon his pursuit.

As Sabikeshiinh kept ramping up the speed of the

scenery changes, and Bugz grew more confident in her skills, the bot was run ragged.

The bot continued his attempted sorties, but Bugz could see that he was losing power and energy with each clumsy attack. While he continued to move with superhuman speed, he was no longer in control. Bugz judged that within a few more strikes, she would either eliminate the bot or Sabikeshiinh would cast him away into the darkness forever.

It was then that Bugz recognized their surroundings had changed from a tunnel of light to aurora borealis.

"Waawaate," she whispered to herself as the bot appeared again before her.

"Yes!" the bot shouted back, grabbing her arms around the biceps. "It's me," he said through his crooked grin. She shook her arms free. In the split second where the bot tumbled away from her, this time likely the last, she recognized the form of her brother—not any particular feature but simply the overall way his body moved, similar to how she would sometimes recognize a friend down the gravel road on the Rez simply by their gait.

Without thinking, she reached for him and grabbed him by both hands. She was instantly transported to a memory of her swimming with her brother as a young child. She'd panicked in the lake water and he'd pulled her onto a dock, saving her.

Now the roles had been reversed.

Bugz felt the continued pull of the realm-changing roiling her body and noted its quickening pace. Clearly Sabikeshiinh could see the bot was no longer a threat, holding hands with Bugz as he was. Yet the spider continued to whip them into a frenzy. Bugz realized this must mean the electrical storm, the northern lights, was the way to destroy the Waawaate-bot once and for all.

All she had to do was let go.

The Waawaate-bot looked down at his feet and then back to Bugz. As he did, his expression changed. He was no longer the deranged tormentor that had pursued her and countless others to the ends of the 'Verse. Instead, Bugz saw the look of a desperate young man.

The bot's mouth was still twisted into an unnatural curl and his teeth were still sharpened to extreme points, but Bugz looked to his hands: they were the strong, brown hands of her brother. Her gaze traveled up his arms and toward the rest of his body: that was her brother's regalia. Finally, her eyes traveled past the crooked smile and found the windows into his soul.

These were her brother's eyes.

As the brilliant purple and green lights shook furiously into pinks and whites, Bugz could feel her heart pounding in time. The storm was becoming more and more intense. It was harder and harder for her to hang on to the Waawaate-bot as Sabikeshiinh worked faster to rid him from the blockchain that powered the Floraverse. Bugz knew what the spider was attempting but kept her eyes locked with those of the bot. There was a sadness deep within those eyes, a sadness she had rarely seen in them before. *How did I make this simulation so real?* she asked herself. The eyes she stared into were dark brown with aurorae dancing upon their surfaces. The brow that framed them rose to its center, telegraphing a form of worry. Regret, to be specific. Bugz had only seen this look on her brother's face one time.

This was the way Waawaate had looked at her the last time she'd spoken to him in the hospital. Weary, sad, defeated, but not yet finished.

Bugz had been completely emotionally exhausted. Helping her brother through that long year of fighting cancer, the visits, the treatments, the vomiting. The ups and downs of him coming home from the hospital only to be sent back again—the stays at home becoming progressively shorter and the trips back longer until, for the final two months, there were no more visits home. The pain she'd witnessed in Waawaate, the pain she'd witnessed in her parents, the pain she'd felt within herself. She'd sung a song on that final day with her brother, the same healing song she'd sung to Waawaate throughout his sickness. He'd closed his eyes while she'd sung, furrowing his brow as though listening intently. He never opened his eyes again.

A tear rolled down Bugz's cheek.

As the northern lights crackled and shook with energy, she held a death grip on the strong brown hands before her. The melody poured from her voice without warning. The words returned to her, too.

"Eniwek igo kiga'onji-pimaadiz ndiwe'igan," she sang, while staring into the eyes that captivated her soul. *Through my drum you will live just a little bit longer.*

Aurorae shimmered brilliantly all around her. Bugz could almost make out the forms of the ancestors dancing in her midst, the ones her parents had explained to her danced in the sky to make the northern lights.

Bugz remembered again the colors of the flooring and the wallpaper in that hospital room—a faded red the color of blood on a sidewalk and a putrid green the color of a wilting mint leaf. Colors she never wanted to see again. Colors she'd been staring at when she heard her brother's heart monitor flatline. Colors she'd kept staring at as a nurse and Feng's aunt Liumei came tearing into the room. Wearing a white coat, with a stethoscope around her neck, Liumei performed all manner of pointless techniques to try to revive Bugz's brother. Finally, framed by those same disgusting reds and greens, Liumei climbed onto the hospital bed and listened intently to the chest of the empty shell that had once been Waawaate. In this memory, as in the real-life event Bugz had witnessed, Liumei raised herself slowly, shaking her head until she finally pronounced Bugz's brother dead.

She remembered the sounds of her mother wailing and Feng crying, how those sounds had swirled around her. Bugz now found herself staring back into those same eyes with the same expression in them as she'd seen on that awful day. She tightened her grip.

Bugz had no way to gauge the passage of time. The northern lights danced furiously around them as though a pow-wow drum group of giants was picking up the beat. The force of the motion Sabikenshiinh propelled them with threatened to tear her arms from her shoulders. The bot itself was babbling something incoherent.

Bugz ignored all of this. She was trapped in that moment with the eyes of her brother. The eyes she'd yearned to see for so long. The feeling they sparked in her heart was a feeling she hadn't known since Waawaate's departure. The familiarity with which they greeted her welcomed her in a way she never wanted to lose again. It had hurt so much to let go of him once already. This felt right. This felt true. This is what she'd been chasing. She'd finally found it. This is why she'd worked so hard to recreate Waawaate in the Floraverse . . . to bring him back from the Spirit World.

And then she remembered.

This was not her brother.

As much as she wanted it to be, it couldn't be. While it may have resembled him, it was only a replica—one that had shown itself to be something very different from the brother she cherished so much.

She clenched her eyes shut at the realization that she wouldn't see her brother again for a very long time.

"Gigawaabamin minawaa, Waawaate," she said, the tears flowing. *I will see you again, Waawaate.*

Bugz released her grip.

The strong brown hands slipped away as she opened her eyes.

Bugz watched as the form of her brother in his grass dance regalia flew rapidly away from her and was struck again and again with bolts of lightning such that he was illuminated with electricity. In a burst of light and energy, the bot was destroyed, a blinding flash testifying to the finality of the event.

Bugz covered her face. She could feel the electrical storm around her slowly dissipating . . . just like the feeling of her brother's touch fading slowly from her hands.

The spider set her down on a beam and she felt a different hand on her shoulder. Bugz turned and found Feng standing before her, nodding his head slowly. He pulled her in and she leaned against his chest.

The two of them stood on a brilliant beam of light, embracing each other against the never-ending expanse of the Dreamcatcher.

CHAPTER 45

Waawaate, the real Waawaate, felt his lungs burn and his legs become heavy as he sprinted up the strawberry mountain underneath the night sky. He ignored his feelings of weariness as the voices of the people grew louder. Their laughter grew closer. His heart filled with joy. He saw the hilltop fall before him as he reached the summit of his journey.

Words cannot do justice to what he saw next.

The sight filled his heart with a happiness that eclipsed the sadness he'd felt throughout his journey on the Path of Souls. This happiness revealed itself to be the missing piece of a puzzle, one that connected all of the challenges and hardships he'd ever known on Earth, which he now understood to be important parts of the journey that had brought him here.

Waawaate felt an urge to look behind him and study the places from which he'd come, but he knew he should not.

Instead, he spoke to those who greeted him. His ancestors. His people. His mother, father, and sister, Stormy, all of whom he could now see perfectly, with only love in his eyes. Everyone who had ever lived and everyone who ever would was there together in that place of timeless eternal bliss.

They took each other's hands and danced together, dancing hard against the brilliant night sky.

"We will be together forever," they sang to each other in the stars.

CHAPTER 46

Shielding her eyes from the golden harvest sun, Bugz looked out past the army of Clan:LESS soldiers in the Floraverse and to the giant stone children carved into the mountainside beyond them. Her first instinct was to fire her laser gun from her hip and take out as many of the clanmates as possible. The centurions, orcs, and ogres in the middle distance seemed to be particularly easy targets, given their size. Bugz pictured them falling one after the other, gamertags rising in white text against the clear blue sky. *But what if I miss them and vandalize Feng's beautiful monument instead?* she asked herself. She glanced at Feng who, seeming to sense her thoughts, furrowed his brow as if to say *knock it off*. She looked back ahead at the Clan:LESS soldiers closest to her. Gym, the Behemoth, Joe. She recognized them as Feng's closest friends. *Well, they used to be his closest friends*, Bugz corrected her internal monologue. These warriors flanked Alpha, who stood directly before Bugz.

Alpha had clearly fallen on hard times. Though he was still a mountain of virtual muscle with the cool facial scar, his hair had grown out . . . and not in a cool way, either. It looked wet and limp, giving him the appearance of a long-haired dog who'd been caught in the rain. Alpha was also only wearing cargo shorts and simple boots. Bugz figured he'd have to take some time to work his way back up to the slick body armor and combat gear she'd seen him in so often.

Alpha's different-colored eyes, brown and green, scanned a formal-looking piece of parchment that he held unspooled in his hands. "So that concludes it," he said, apparently continuing a conversation to which Bugz hadn't been paying attention. "We've added that provision about not returning to the nests in the 'Verse or in the real world, or telling anyone about where they are currently . . ." Alpha looked up. "So we have a deal?"

Bugz nodded.

"Alright then, let's get this signed. Gym, table, please." At this, Gym snapped his fingers and two orcs ambled forward with a large oak desk, setting it down before their boss. Alpha leaned forward, spreading the parchment across the wooden surface. He signed his name with a plume he'd dipped in ink. "Your turn," he said, turning the paper to Bugz. She inhaled sharply and stepped forward.

Bugz looked at the document and read the title

written in Olde English font across the top aloud. "Peace Treaty." She shot a look to Feng, who only sucked his teeth and shrugged. She looked out at the horde in front of her before bringing her gaze back to the soldiers and leader across from her. She looked at the massive stone children in the distance. She thought about the inheritance they represented, the sacrifice they'd made so she could practice the Anishinaabe culture, the same culture she'd shared with the entire Floraverse. They'd endured so much just so she could be who she was.

Bugz nodded her head slowly and decided to sign. If nothing else, she could use this document to prove Clan:LESS's treachery should they ever renege on its terms. With a few swipes, she scrawled a picture of a pelican, her clan animal, across the parchment and pushed it back across the table.

Alpha rolled the treaty up and paused for a moment, clutching the tube in his hands. "You know, Bugz, I just want to say thanks." He pursed his lips as he paused. "I know we haven't always gotten along. We may have said some things. You've said some things."

Bugz rolled her eyes at the "both-sides-ism" that was happening.

"But I'm glad you were able to stop the bot," Alpha continued. "I mean, we wouldn't be able to play the game again if you hadn't. Nobody would've been able to use the Floraverse again. Ever. So no more hostilities—either here, or in the real world."

At this, the eight-foot-tall warlord nodded, turned on his heels, and followed his troops, who began a march toward the sunset. Bugz stood silently next to Feng, studying the horde as they made their way across a golden meadow.

When the army was out of earshot, she spoke. "I'm not sure about this deal."

"I don't trust them for a second," Feng responded. "But at least they promised no court action. That should hold up in the real world."

"It's not that. Well, I mean, that's fine." Bugz looked to Feng to see if he shared her nervousness. She saw no sign of it. "It's just, isn't it kind of messed up?"

"What?"

"Creating the bot was bad. It was terrible. I feel awful about it." She watched Feng bite his lip in contemplation. "And yet, they're willing to reward me with this . . . I'm having a hard time saying the word 'treaty,' by the way . . . but they're rewarding me with this deal, even though I did something so bad." She shook her head and looked down at her floral moccasins. Bugz suddenly felt a vague sense of guilt.

"You're overthinking it. Just be glad you've got one less thing to worry about."

Her anxiety rushed to fill the void. Bugz's thoughts returned to the traitor and the comment section. "Well, even if Clan:LESS is going to chill for now, what about the hater?"

"She's already posted a video saying what you did to get rid of the bot was pretty cool." Feng cleared his throat. "Now that everyone can use the 'Verse again, I guess she's bragging about how long she's known you and how she always believed you had this in you. She's never been so happy." Feng shook his head, smiling. "Who knew you'd even wind up saving *her*, too?"

Bugz grinned.

Feng's smile widened, happy that he'd finally gotten Bugz to lighten up. "There's my girl," he said. Feng glanced at his feet and drew a breath before looking into Bugz's eyes again. "The girl that I love."

Bugz could feel herself blushing, though she had no idea whether her 'Versona's appearance reflected this. "Thanks," she said softly, flashing a brilliant smile that radiated with the joy she felt inside.

Stepping forward, Bugz wrapped her arms around Feng.

"I love you too," she said.

They kissed each other as the setting sun wrapped them in a golden glow, two beings haloed as one by the light of their virtual world. The giant stone children looked out over Bugz and Feng, their rock faces beaming.

CHAPTER 47

The fire crackled and sent a column of sparks spiraling to the heavens, their orange embers contrasting vividly with the night sky. Bugz hugged herself in her hoodie and looked over at Stormy, who sat on a lawn chair beside her, staring contentedly into the fire in front of them. Bugz looked to Feng, who sat across from them, and back at the flames, studying the blue and white glow of the rocks buried in the heart of the blaze. They'd be going into the Sweat Lodge soon.

"So you saved the 'Verse for all of us." Stormy's eyes smiled. "That's pretty awesome. You're a hero for real, Bugz."

Bugz felt a pang of shyness and shook her head. "I had to." She found a smile still on Stormy's face. "I just wish others hadn't been hurt along the way. I guess I should've known not to reach across the Spirit World—"

Stormy interrupted. "Girl, I know we talked about bad medicine and crooked mouths and all that stuff before. But that is not why the bot went haywire." Bugz studied her friend's expression as Stormy continued to watch the blaze. Bugz tried to discern whether Stormy really believed these words or was merely trying to reassure her. Stormy spoke again. "Maybe you're just not as good at building stuff in the 'Verse as you think you are." The friends laughed together. The fire popped again and more sparks showered the sky. "It's okay, Bugz. You've had a hard year." Stormy cleared her throat. "We all have."

Bugz's father came from the house carrying a pail of steaming cedar water. His mother followed with a plate of strawberries.

"Well, the rocks are pretty much ready to go. We can go in as soon as Liumei gets here," Bugz's father said.

"I'm not sure I'm going in, Dad."

"Why not?"

"I'm just not sure I'm feeling it."

"Is this about the people talking online?" Frank looked back and forth between Stormy and Bugz before speaking again. "You know, Bugz, don't let the haters get you down. Besides, I hear the culture police are claiming to be your friends now." He smiled and wiped the sweat from his brow. Glancing at Bugz, he spoke again. "The Elders never set a specific rule for how long we're supposed to stay away from ceremony while we're grieving, because it depends on the person. They're only trying to encourage us to be patient with ourselves. Sometimes people rush back into ceremonies, and take all that on, and don't actually take time to mourn their loved one." Frank placed the bucket inside the sweat and turned back to face the fire. "But I think you've done everything right, and I think we're doing the right thing by going into the sweat tonight, too. We're helping each other through a tough time and there's nothing wrong with that." He stared into the blaze.

"Bugz, forgive the haters, for they know not what they do," Stormy said through a grin.

Bugz felt lighter. Still, all she could articulate in this moment was a soft "alright." She turned to Stormy. "You ready to go in then, girl?"

"I don't think I'll be coming in tonight." Stormy shifted in her chair, appearing self-conscious in the light of the fire, and looked down toward the blanket that wrapped her legs.

"Oh. You know, you're welcome to join us . . ." Bugz's mother looked to her husband and back to Stormy. "No matter what."

"No, I know." Stormy stared at her legs and flicked a firefly from the blanket. "Actually, there's something I need to tell you folks."

Bugz glanced to her parents, who looked expectantly at Stormy. She followed their gaze.

"Well." Stormy drew in a deep breath and huffed it out quickly, wiping something from the corner of her eye. Bugz noted the length of her eyelashes—they only accentuated the beauty of Stormy's hazelnut eyes. Stormy cleared her throat again. "I'm pregnant."

"Congratulations, girl!" Bugz's mother said as she rushed forward and leaned in for a hug.

"That's a blessing," Bugz's father said, patting Stormy on the shoulder. "You can still come in the lodge though—you know that, right? You've got plenty to pray for now."

"I know." Stormy smiled widely, flashing straight white teeth. "I just feel a little . . . off."

"Morning sickness." Bugz's mother returned the smile.

"Yup." Stormy looked away, apparently overcome by shyness.

Bugz asked how far along Stormy was and grew silent when she heard the reply—three months. She started doing the math in her head. Quickly, she looked back to Stormy. Their eyes met and Stormy smiled wider still as a tear fell down her cheek.

"Who is the father?" Feng said, oblivious to the silent communication going on in front of him.

Brushing the back of her hand beneath her eye, Stormy sniffed and chuckled. "I don't know how tell you this, Mr. and Mrs. Holiday. Bugz. I love you guys so much and I don't want to put anything on you, because you've been through so much already, but I just want you to know . . ." She breathed deeply again and looked to Frank and Summer hopefully. "The baby is your son's. I'm carrying your grandchild."

Bugz felt overcome as all the sadness, joy, grief, and laughter she'd known recently washed over her. She bit her bottom lip, hoping it would help. She looked into the fire as she heard her mother and father make their way to Stormy and wrap her with praise, gratitude, and love. They lifted Stormy up out of her seat with hugs and a warm familial embrace.

"Come here, Buggy," her father beckoned. His outstretched hand waved her in.

Bugz stood and walked over to her family, her family that was now growing again. Bugz wrapped her arms around Stormy and buried her face in her friend's hair. Bugz whimpered as she let the tears flow. Stormy returned the embrace and rubbed Bugz's shoulders.

Composing herself, Bugz stepped back and stood beside Stormy as her parents bookended the pair. Feng stood as well, offering Stormy a hug too. Together they remained silent, save for the sounds of the fire that roared before them. After a long while, Stormy spoke again.

"I'm going to name the baby Waawaate." Stormy smiled, two tiny reflections of the fire burning in her eyes. Bugz's parents exclaimed their gratitude, while all Bugz could do was try to hold herself together. Stormy continued. "I'm going to name the baby Waawaate . . . to show how we're all carrying on. Carrying on this sacred journey . . ." She nodded, smiling serenely. "On the Everlasting Road."

Bugz looked to the sky above, suddenly feeling tiny before the majesty of the universe. She drew the smoke-scented air in deeply and made out the stars shining in the dark sky above her. As she exhaled, she could see the Milky Way set distantly into the darkness behind the stars. Her heart reached into this expanse.

Bugz raised her arms to the sky and formed the hand symbol for the heart. Staring at the faraway lights through the space between her grips, she slowly raised her thumbs until her hands formed the never-ending loop of the infinity symbol. She thought of the path her brother was walking somewhere far away. She thought of the path she was walking here on Earth. She released her hands and brought her arms back down to her sides.

Bugz, still looking to the heavens, nodded and repeated Stormy's words. "The Everlasting Road." She shook her head and spoke again. "Brother, brother, brother . . ."

ACKNOWLEDGMENTS

Miigwech apichi, a huge amount of gratitude to my wife, Lisa, and our kids, Dom, Bezh, and Toba. I couldn't have written this book without your love and support. Thanks so much for all the laughs, dinner table conversations, and inspiration that provided the fuel for me to write this novel. Another big miigwech to my younger sister Shawon, who really helped me talk through and understand the character Bugz. I also want to thank my mom, who helps us so much every day, and my late dad. I feel like I won the lottery to be raised by the two of you. Much love to my sisters Kiizh, Diane, and Pat, as well as to April and all of our extended family. And to our Sundance family, I missed you so much during the pandemic times. I will see you all again soon at the center of the center of the universe.

Ginanaakomininim, many thanks, to the readers who helped to improve this book; namely, Lisa, C.B. Lee,

Mark Rosner, and Tasha Spillett. Tasha, you've been such a huge help beyond just reading, but really in offering counsel as I've written this; I want to give an extra shout out to you, Len, and Izzy. Miigwech!

Thank you to two of the best editors anyone could hope to work with: Lynne Missen and Peter Phillips. You've helped bring better and better versions out of each subsequent draft and you did so in such a kind and generous way. Thank you Linda Pruessen for the thoughtful and insightful copyedit, and to proofreader Erin Kern. My sincere gratitude to my one-of-a-kind literary agent, Jackie Kaiser, for your help in publishing the books in this series, as well as to everyone at Westwood Creative Artists for your help and support. Thanks to Jay Soule for the beautiful cover art. Once again, you've really helped bring the characters and this story to life!

I would also like to acknowledge the late Gregory Younging for the seminal text *Elements of Indigenous Style*, whose principles were wonderful guidance for this book. Miigwech again to Niigaan Sinclair and Tasha Spillett for additional insight into those approaches. Mársi cho to T'áncháy Redvers for the generosity in helping me compile the resources listed in the following pages and for breaking a trail in creating culturally safe spaces for youth.

Thank you, Mr. Mehmet Tohti, for the important work you do with the Uyghur Rights Advocacy Project and to bring attention to the plight of your people. We must ensure the human rights of the Uyghur people are respected.

My heart is full of good feeling and gratitude for all the good people I've crossed paths with in the book world along the way, including Evan Munday, Nicole Winstanley, Diane Turbide, Stephen Myers, Patrick Crean, Tara Mora, Erin Balser, Ann Jansen, Shelagh Rogers, and the Canada Reads team, among many others.

To the students at Pelican Falls First Nations High School: as I wrote in *Walking in Two Worlds*, I was first inspired to write this series when I met some of you a few years back and noticed many of you reading young adult novels. I hope this novel gives you some positive things you can take with you on your journeys. Your inspiration has been such a wonderful gift in the form of writing these books and getting to know the characters in them. And thanks for the hoodie! I liked it so much I wore it in the author photo for this book.

To everyone else who has taken the time to read this novel—I hope you take something positive from it. It's certainly been a great opportunity to commit these words to the page. I am so very grateful to have the opportunity to share this series with the world. It has truly been a blessing in my life. Miigwech!

RESOURCES

Culturally Safe Resources in Canada

We Matter is an Indigenous youth-led movement that has videos, toolkits, and resources for Indigenous youth in all provinces and territories. Find them at wemattercampaign.org.

Hope for Wellness Help Line is a 24/7 national helpline for Indigenous people experiencing distress, dealing with traumas, or just needing to talk. Call 1-855-242-3310 or chat online at hopeforwellness.ca. Available in French, English, Anishinaabemowin, Cree, and Inuktitut.

Talk 4 Healing is a helpline for Indigenous women and girls in Ontario. Call 1-855-554-HEAL 24/7 or chat online at talk4healing.com for help with crisis, cultural supports, and healing.

KUU-US Crisis Line (BC) is reachable at 1-800-588-8717 and available 24/7. It offers culturally safe supports for crisis, addictions, and intergenerational trauma. The youth line is 1-250-723-2040. Find them online at kuu-uscrisisline.com.

The **Nunavut Kamatsiaqtut Helpline** is available at 1-800-265-3333 if you just want to talk, are in crisis, or are worried about someone you care about. The service is available in English, French, and Inuktitut. Their website is nunavuthelpline.ca.

LGBT Youth Line is not a crisis line but is a youth-led LGBTQ2S+ resource. Text 1-647-694-4275 or head to youthline.ca to chat online.

Kids Help Phone is available 24/7 across Canada at 1-800-668-6868, or you can text 686868. Their website is kidshelpphone.ca.

CULTURALLY SAFE RESOURCES IN THE UNITED STATES

The **National Suicide Prevention Lifeline** is available 24/7 at 1-800-273-8255. They have Indigenous-specific resources at suicidepreventionlifeline.org and are a safe space for LGBTQ2S+ callers.

The **Crisis Text Line** is also available 24/7. If you're in crisis, text HOME to 741741 to contact a counsellor for free. You can text from the United States or Canada, or message them on Facebook. Their website is crisistextline.org.

Teen Line supports teens in crisis, those with mental health needs, or those who just want to talk about problems with someone other than friends and parents. Call 1-800-TLC-TEEN (1-800-852-8336) or text 839863. Find out more on their website at teenlineonline.org.

We R Native is an online resource for Indigenous youth in the United States that includes cultural resources, sexuality resources, resources for suicide prevention, and more. Text 9779 to follow them, or go to wernative.org for more info.

TrevorLifeLine is a crisis line that helps LGBTQ2S+ youth. Call 1-866-488-7386, text START to 678678, or chat online at thetrevorproject.org.

Strong Hearts Helpline offers support for Indigenous people in the United States who've experienced gender-based or sexual violence. Call 1-844-762-8483 or chat online at strongheartshelpline.org.

You Are Not Alone Network lists crisis lines for many tribes at youarenotalonenetwork.org.